C000192567

Bon Bons, Bourbon and Bon Mots:

Stories from the Algonquin Round Table

The Early Writing of:

Franklin Pierce Adams
Robert Benchley
Heywood Broun
Edna Ferber
Ruth Hale
Dorothy Parker
Donald Ogden Stewart

Traveling Press
Special Edition Books

Bon Bons, Bourbon and Bon Mots:
Stories from the Algonquin Round Table

By Franklin Pierce Adams, Robert Benchley, Heywood Broun, Edna Ferber, Ruth Hale, Dorothy Parker, Donald Ogden Stewart

Introduction by Laura Bonds
Edited by Laura Bonds, Shawn Conners

Additional biographical data for Robert Benchley provided by Nat Benchley.

Second Edition – January, 2011

Published by
Traveling Press
El Paso, Texas USA

ISBN10 1-934255-34-3
ISBN13 978-1-934255-34-6

Printed in the United States of America

CONTENTS

Introduction

"Silly of me to blame it on dates, but so it happened to be. Dammit, it was the Twenties, and we had to be smarty." –
Dorothy Parker

The Algonquin Round Table, or "The Vicious Circle" as it was commonly known, came about much like so many ordinary weekly poker games or monthly book clubs or Sunday brunch gatherings tend to. A few friends get together, have a good time, and decide it would be fun to do it on a regular basis. Now, age these friends in their twenties. Give them all literary or theatrical pedigrees, larger than life personalities and untold amounts of alcohol. Then put them in a time and place that encourages artistic creativity, outrageous behavior, and the breaking of social norms. Lastly, give them national exposure. What emerges is a group that not only sets the standard for contemporary literary style and wit, but helps change forever the face of American culture.

1919, the year following the end of World War I, found three young aspiring writers working together at the offices of *Vanity Fair* in New York City. Movie critic Robert E. Sherwood, theater critic Dorothy Parker, and managing editor Robert Benchley found instant camaraderie with each other, and the friends would often lunch together at the Algonquin Hotel located a few doors down from the magazine's headquarters.

Sometime in June of that year, John Peter Toohey, writer, publicist, and associate of the *Vanity Fair* trio, cooked up an idea for a practical joke to be played on *New York Times* drama critic and contemporary Alexander Wollcott. Wollcott was returning from the Great War after working as a correspondent for the military newspaper *Stars and Stripes*. Toohey was annoyed at Wollcott for not plugging one of the publicist's clients in his newspaper column. Under the guise of a surprise luncheon to welcome Wollcott back stateside, Toohey gathered together the group that would form the core of the Round Table and commenced a roast poking fun of the critic on a number of fronts. The event was such a success, and Wollcott enjoyed the joke so thoroughly, that Toohey suggested that the group begin to meet at the Algonquin, or "The Gonk," for lunch on a daily basis. Thus The Vicious Circle was born.

Only it didn't quite start out as a circle. The group first gathered at a long rectangular table situated in the Algonquin's Pergola Room (now The Oak Room). The hotel's first general manager, Frank Case, was known to curry favor with people from the worlds of publishing and theater, and he welcomed the young up-and-comers with open arms. In fact, Case would provide the low-paid writers free celery and popovers to help ensure their return visits. As membership increased, Case eventually moved them to the Rose Room and sat them at a large, round table. Initially, they referred to themselves simply as "The Board." Once they were assigned their own waiter named Luigi, they became "The Luigi Board." One day, Dorothy Parker christened them a "vicious circle," and the name stuck, though The Round Table was most often used by the public, so-called after a caricature was published of the group sitting at a round table, wearing armor.

In addition to Parker, Benchley, Sherwood, Toohey and Woollcott, the core group consisted of columnist Franklin P. Adams, columnist and sportswriter Heywood Broun, playwright Marc Connelly, playwright and director George S. Kaufman, and journalist Harold Ross. Membership was not fixed, so many other luminaries moved in and out of the Circle, such as author and playwright Edna Ferber, playwright and screenwriter Donald Ogden Stewart, journalist and feminist (and wife to Broun) Ruth Hale, composer Deems Taylor, writer and historian Margaret Leech, actresses Peggy Wood and Tallulah Bankhead, actor and comedian Harpo Marx, and many others. All told, there were more than 30 members to grace the table at the Algonquin during the course of the ten-year lunch.

The associations of the members went well beyond the daily lunches, however. Many of them, such as Parker and Benchley, already worked with each other. But if they didn't work together, they all most assuredly played together. Great fans of games, several of the Circle formed a regular Saturday night poker club, dubbing themselves the Thanatopsis Literary and Inside Straight Club. Other games in the group's regular rotation were cribbage, charades, and something called the "I can give you a sentence" game, which reportedly spawned Dorothy Parker's famous use of the word *horticulture*: "You can lead a horticulture, but you can't make her think." As if all of this conviviality weren't enough, several of the Algonks also co-owned a small private island in the middle of a lake in Vermont where they would go to visit and play croquet.

The Round Table was certainly composed of people with a shared admiration of each other's work – some might have argued too much admiration. But it was in this mutual esteem that the members were able to help one another get their careers up and running. Many of them had newspaper or magazine columns, and as they would trade quips, they would freely quote each other to find their wisecracks in the papers the next day. Most notably, Franklin P. Adams would use his popular column "The Conning Tower" to promote the cutting remarks and witty light verse of his fellow crew. It was with this exposure that many of the Round Tablers got their first real taste of national recognition and fame, and not only with the reading public. It has been said that the writings and opinions of the members also had strong influence on emerging writers F. Scott Fitzgerald and Ernest Hemingway.

It would seem inevitable a group with such literary proclivities and tight-knit relations would eventually collaborate on a cohesive work of their own. Indeed they did, and that work took the shape of 1922's *No, Sirree!*, a nonsensical one-night-only theatrical revue. The production was essentially a response to theater producers who were incensed by bitingly poor reviews issued by the critics' faction of the Circle, and who challenged the group to come up with something better themselves. The revue was a relative hit, featuring acts written and performed entirely by Round Tablers, with Robert Benchley's contribution "The Treasurer's Report" garnering the most praise. Buoyed by the success of *No, Sirree!*, the group attempted to repeat their achievement with an "official" Vicious Circle production to be performed by professional actors. The revue, named *The Forty-niners*, opened in November 1922, and turned out to be a flop, running only 15 weeks before production was closed.

Undeterred by the failure, members of the Round Table continued to collaborate on different projects in addition to pursuing their individual careers. Of particular note is the book *Nonsenseorship*, published in 1922. Several in the Circle were known for their outspoken views regarding social justice and personal freedoms, as well as a deep appreciation of the consumption of alcohol. The Roaring Twenties was an era defined by social and societal upheaval, one that not only gave rise to the women's rights movement, but also to Prohibition and other forms of censorship. Parker, Woollcott, Hale, and

4

Broun all contributed essays to *Nonsenseorship*, a manifesto that challenged what much of the intelligentsia of the era saw as the oppressions of the decade, especially the ban on liquor.

Of course, the Round Tablers continued to lunch. As the antics and outrageous behavior of the group grew in notoriety, their names became known nationwide, and by 1925, The Vicious Circle was out-and-out famous. What had begun as a private clique had become public amusement, with people often inquiring of the Algonquin staff who of the Circle was at lunch that day. Some just came in and stared. America was enthralled by their discussions, debates, jokes, opinions, and sound bites.

Not everyone was a fan of the group, however. Many contemporaries were critics, accusing the members of cronyism and insular favoritism. James Thurber, a long-time detractor, felt that the Round Tablers were too consumed by their own practical jokes to be taken seriously by anyone in the literary world. Groucho Marx, brother to Harpo, commented disparagingly of the group: "The price of admission is a serpent's tongue and a half-concealed stiletto." Even the Circle's own members were known to denigrate their association. Edna Ferber called them "The Poison Squad" and wrote that "they were actually merciless if they disapproved. I have never encountered a more hard-bitten crew." She did credit them however, and went on to say "if they liked what you had done, they did say so publicly and whole-heartedly." Dorothy Parker, arguably the Round Table's most vital member, was even more critical, saying later in her life that the group "was just a lot of people telling jokes and telling each other how good they were. Just a bunch of loudmouths showing off... There was no truth in anything they said."

Despite Parker's dismissal of the group's importance, it remains that the contributions of the Round Table members have added significantly and enduringly to the literary and cultural landscape. Harold Ross used his associations with the Tablers to get his cosmopolitan magazine *The New Yorker*, of which he was editor until his death, off the ground. Kaufman, Connelly, Sherwood, and Ferber all produced Pulitzer Prize-winning work. Several of the group made their way to Hollywood to write Oscar-winning screenplays or produce award winning films. Parker herself remains celebrated for her short stories, poems and literary reviews.

As the 1930s approached and members of the Round Table started to find opportunities outside of New York City, the bonds that held the group together inevitably began to loosen. "It didn't end, it just sort of faded," recalled Marc Connelly. Edna Ferber had said she realized it was over the day she showed up at the Algonquin for lunch one day in 1932 and found a family from Kansas seated at the group's usual table. Naturally, some members remained friends after the group's dissolution, particularly Parker and Benchley, but for all intents and purposes, the Vicious Circle had been broken. For one glorious decade, however, the country was treated to the biting wit and sparkling wordplay of a band of tastemakers who embodied an era and enduringly affected American humor.

What follows in these pages is a collection of stories, poems, and essays taken from seven of the more prolific members of The Algonquin Round Table: Donald Ogden Stewart, Robert Benchley, Dorothy Parker, Franklin Pierce Adams, Heywood Broun, Ruth Hale, and Edna Ferber. All of the pieces represent the writers' earlier work, either right before or just as The Vicious Circle began its rise to fame, and placing all of these written works in the public domain.

6

Without a doubt, the sharp wit and sarcasm that defined the spirit of the Round Table abounds in this volume. What the reader will also find are glimpses of the earnest writers that lived behind the joker's masks. Parker's short story, "Such a Pretty Little Picture," reveals a kind of tender sincerity not often found in her poems. Ruth Hale's essay, "The Woman's Place," her contribution to *Nonsenseorship*, is a no-holds-barred representation of some of the group's fierce dedication to exposing the social ills of the era. The short stories of Edna Ferber are perhaps the most literary pieces of the bunch, written with a vivid style and substantive view of contemporary society.

The Algonquin Round Table as a whole may have been most famous for their off-the-cuff barbs and cutting remarks made over lunch. What each member of this true artist's community gave in literary gems, however, has left a legacy unmatched in modern American culture. Cheers!

Laura Bonds, April 2010

Stories from the Algonquin Round Table

Donald Ogden Stewart

1894–1980

Author, playwright and screenwriter Donald Ogden Stewart was born in Columbus, Ohio. After graduating from Yale University, Stewart enlisted in the U.S. Naval Reserves, serving during World War I. After his military service ended, Stewart spent some years traveling in Europe until he finally settled in New York, where he began his writing career penning satirical novels. He found early success in 1921 with *A Parody Outline of History*, a satire of H.G. Wells' *The Outline of History*. This success led to friendships with the likes of Dorothy Parker, Robert Benchley, and George S. Kaufman, and consequently, membership into the Algonquin Round Table. He also befriended Ernest Hemingway, who modeled the character Bill Gorton in *The Sun Also Rises* after Stewart.

In 1928, Stewart was introduced to the theater by an old college friend who had written a part in a Broadway play with Stewart in mind. After taking the part and being bitten by the stage bug, Stewart wrote and starred in his first play, *Rebound*, in 1930, followed by a musical, *Fine and Dandy*, the same year.

As early as 1925, Stewart had become interested in adapting some of his own novels for the screen, but instead had to adapt the works of others as his projects were initially shelved. In 1930, he moved to Hollywood and had a small part in the film *Not So Dumb*, but his passion remained screenwriting. Stewart soon began to build a reputation for writing sophisticated screenplays with a master's touch for dialogue. Among his better known film scripts are *The*

9

Prisoner of Zenda, *Love Affair*, *Kitty Foyle*, and *Life with Father*, but Stewart is best known for his screenplay adaptation of *The Philadelphia Story*, for which he won the Academy Award. This classic 1940 screwball comedy, starring Katherine Hepburn, Cary Grant, and James Stewart, is still cited of as one of the greatest movies of the 20th Century for its sizzling wit and firecracker dialogue. A second Academy Award was given to James Stewart for his performance in *The Philadelphia Story*, which the actor accepted with humility, indicating he didn't consider himself deserving of the award. Donald Ogden Stewart, on the other hand, declared upon winning his Oscar: "I have no one to thank but myself!"

When World War II began and Hitler's rise to power escalated, Stewart became an active member of Hollywood's Anti-Nazi League, an association that would come back to haunt him later in the McCarthy era. During the Second Red Scare, it was claimed that the organization had been a cover-up for a Communist cell. Stewart was blacklisted in 1950, left Hollywood in 1951, and immigrated to London. He stayed in England for the rest of his life, as the U.S. State Department refused to renew his passport, considering him a threat to U.S. security. In 1975, Stewart wrote his memoir, *By a Stroke of Luck*. Donald Ogden Stewart died in London at the age of 85, survived by his wife of 40 years, Ella, who died later the same year.

MAIN STREET: PLYMOUTH, MASS.

In the manner of Sinclair Lewis

I

1620.

Late autumn.

The sour liver-colored shores of America.

Breaking waves dashing too high on a stern and rockbound coast.

Woods tossing giant branches planlessly against a stormy sky.

Cape Cod Bay — wet and full of codfish. The codfish — wet and full of bones.

Standing on the deck of the anchored "Mayflower," gazing reflectively at the shores of the new world, is Priscilla Kennicott.

A youthful bride on a ship full of pilgrims; a lily floating in a dish of prunes; a cloisonné vase in a cargo of oil cans.

Her husband joins her. Together they go forward to where their fellow pilgrims are preparing to embark in small boats.

Priscilla jumps into the bow of the first of these to shove off.

As the small craft bumps the shore, Priscilla rises joyously. She stretches her hands in ecstasy toward the new world. She leans forward against the breeze, her whole figure alive with the joy of expectant youth.

She leaps with an irrepressible "Yippee!" from the boat to the shore.

She remains for an instant, a vibrant pagan, drunk with the joy of life; Pan poised for an unforgettable moment on Plymouth Rock.

The next minute her foot slips on the hard, wet, unyielding stone. She clutches desperately. She slides slowly back into the cold chill saltiness of Cape Cod Bay.

She is pulled, dripping and ashamed, into the boat. She crouches there, shivering and hopeless. She hears someone whisper, "Pride goeth before destruction, and a haughty spirit before a fall."

A coarse mirthless chuckle.

The pilgrims disembark.

II

Plymouth.

A year later.

Night.

She lay sleepless on her bed.

She heard the outside door open; Kennicott returning from prayer meeting.

He sat down on the bed and began pulling off his boots. She knew that the left boot would stick. She knew exactly what he would say and how long it would take him to get it off. She rolled over in bed, a tactical movement which left no blanket for her husband.

Stories from the Algonquin Round Table

"You weren't at prayer meeting," he said.

"I had a headache," she lied. He expressed no sympathy.

"Miles Standish was telling me what you did today at the meeting of the Jolly Seventeen." He had got the boot off at last; he lay down beside her and pulled all the blankets off her onto himself.

"That was kind of Miles." She jerked at the covers but he held them tight. "What charming story did he tell this time?"

"Now look here, Prissie — Miles Standish isn't given to fabrication. He said you told the Jolly Seventeen that next Thanksgiving they ought to give a dance instead of an all-day prayer service."

"Well — anything else?" She gave a tremendous tug at the bedclothes and Kennicott was uncovered again.

"He said you suggested that they arrange a series of lectures on modern religions, and invite Quakers and other radicals to speak right here in Plymouth and tell us all about their beliefs. And not only that but he said you suggested sending a message to the Roman Catholic exiles from England, inviting them to make their home with us. You must have made quite a little speech."

"Well this is the land of religious freedom, isn't it? That's what you came here for, didn't you?" She sat up to deliver this remark — a movement which enabled Kennicott to win back seven-eighths of the bed covering.

"Now look here, Prissie — I'm not narrow like some of these pilgrims who came over with us. But I won't have my wife intimating that a Roman Catholic or a Quaker should be allowed to spread his heresies broadcast in this country. It's all right for you and me to know something about those things, but we must

13

protect our children and those who have not had our advantages. The only way to meet this evil is to stamp it out, quick, before it can get a start. And it's just such so-called broadminded thinkers as you that encourage these heretics. You'll be criticizing the Bible next, I suppose."

Thus in early times did the pious Right Thinkers save the land from Hellfire and Damnation; thus the great-grandfathers of middle-western congressmen; thus the ancestors of platitudinous editorial writers, Sitters on Committees, and tin-horn prohibitionists.

Kennicott got up to cool his wrath and indignation with a drink of water. He stumbled over a chair, reached for the jug, took a drink, set the jug down, stumbled over the same chair, and crawled back into bed. His expedition cost him the loss of all bed covering; he gave up the fight.

"Aside from dragging my own private views over the coals of your righteousness, did you and your friends find anything equally pleasant and self-satisfying to discuss this evening?"

"Eh — what's that? Why, yes, we did. We decided to refuse permission for one of these traveling medicine shows to operate in Plymouth."

"Medicine shows?"

"Yes — you know — like a fair in England. This one claims to come from down south somewhere. 'Smart Set Medicine Show' it's called, run by a fellow named Mencken. Sells cheap whisky to the Indians — makes them crazy, they say. He's another one of your radical friends we don't want around."

"Yes, he might cut in on your own trading with the Indians."

"Oh, for heaven's sake, Prissie — hire a hall."

Silence. He began to snore.

She lay there, sleepless and open-eyed. The clock struck eleven.

"Why can't I get to sleep?"

("Did Will put the cat out?")

"I wonder what this medicine show is like?"

"What is the matter with these people?"

("Or is it me?")

She reached down, pulled the blankets from under her, spread them carefully over the sleeping Kennicott, patting them down affectionately.

The next day she learned what the medicine show was like. She also learned what was the matter with the pilgrims.

III

Morning.

A fog horn.

A fog horn blowing unceasingly.

At breakfast Kennicott pointed with his fork in the direction of the persistent sound.

"There's your Smart Set Medicine Show," he said glumly. "He doesn't seem to care much whether we give him a permit or not."

Then, a minute later, "We'll have to let him stay. Won't do to have the Indians down on us. But I tell you this, Priscilla, I don't want you to go."

"But Will —"

"Prissie, please! I'm sorry I said what I did last night. I was tired. But don't you see, well, I can't just exactly explain — but this fog horn sort of scares me — I don't like it —"

He suddenly rose and put both hands on her shoulders. He looked into her eyes. He leaned over and kissed her on the forehead. He picked up his hat and was gone. It was five minutes before Priscilla noticed that his breakfast had been left untouched.

A fog horn, sounding unceasingly.

She listlessly put away the breakfast dishes. She tried to drown out the sound by singing hymns. She fell on her knees and tried to pray. She found her prayers keeping time to the rise and fall of the notes of that horn. She determined to go out in the air — to find her husband — to go to church, anywhere — as far as possible from the Smart Set Medicine Show.

So she went out the back door and ran as fast as she could toward the place from which came the sound of the fog horn.

IV

An open space on the edge of the forest.

In the center of the clearing a small gaudily-painted tent.

Seated on the ground in a semicircle before the tent, some forty or fifty Indians.

Standing on a box before the entrance to the tent, a man of twenty-five or fifty.

In his left hand he holds a fog horn; in his right, a stein of beer.

He puts the horn to his lips and blows heavy blast.

He bellows, "Beauty − Beauty − Beauty!"

He takes a drink of beer.

He repeats this performance nine times.

He takes up some mud and deftly models the features of several well-known characters − statesmen, writers, critics. In many cases the resemblance is so slight that Priscilla can hardly recognize the character.

He picks up a heavy club and proceeds to beat each one of his modeled figures into a pulp.

The Indians applaud wildly.

He pays no attention to this applause.

He clears his throat and begins to speak. Priscilla is so deafened by the roar of his voice that she cannot hear what he says. Apparently he is introducing somebody; somebody named George.

George steps out of the tent, but does not bow to the audience. In one hand he carries a fencing foil, well constructed, of European workmanship; in his other hand he holds a number of pretty toy balloons which he has made himself.

17

He smiles sarcastically, tosses the balloons into the air, and cleverly punctures them one by one with his rapier.

At each "pop" the announcer blows a loud blast on the fog horn.

When the last balloon has been punctured George retires without acknowledging the applause of the Indians.

The next act is announced as Helen of Troy in "Six Minutes of Beauty." Priscilla learns from the announcer that "this little lady is out of 'Irony' by Theodore Dreiser."

"All ready, Helen —"

The "little lady" appears.

She is somewhat over six feet six in height and built like a boilermaker. She is dressed in pink tights.

"Six Minutes of Beauty" begins when Helen picks up three large iron cannon balls and juggles them. She tosses them in the air and catches them cleverly on the back of her neck.

The six minutes are brought to a successful conclusion when Helen, hanging head downward by one foot from a trapeze, balances lighted lamp on the other foot and plays Beethoven's Fifth Symphony on the slide trombone.

The announcer then begins his lecture. Priscilla has by this time gotten used to the overpowering roar of his voice and she discovers that once this difficulty is overcome she is tremendously impressed by his words.

She becomes more and more attracted to the man. She listens, fascinated, as his lecture draws to a close and he offers his medicine for sale. She presses forward through the crowd of

18

Indians surrounding the stand. She reaches the tent. She gives her coin and receives in return a bottle. She hides it in her cape and hurries home.

She slips in the back way; she pours some of the medicine into a glass; she drinks it.

V

A terrible overwhelming nausea. Vomiting, which lasts for agonizing minutes, leaving her helpless on the floor.

Then cessation.

Then light — blinding light.

VI

At 3:10 Priscilla drank the Mencken medicine; at 3:12 she was lying in agony on the floor; at 3:20 she opened her eyes; at 3:21 she walked out of her front door; and at 3:22 she discovered what was wrong with Plymouth and the pilgrims.

Main Street. Straight and narrow. A Puritan thoroughfare in a Puritan town.

The church. A center of Puritan worship. The shrine of a narrow theology which persistently repressed beauty and joy and life.

The Miles Standish house. The house of a Puritan. A squat, unlovely symbol of repression. Beauty crushed by Morality.

Plymouth Rock. Hard, unyielding — like the Puritan moral code. A huge tombstone on the grave of Pan.

She fled home. She flung herself, sobbing, on the bed. She cried, "They're all Puritans that's what they are, Puritans!"

After a while she slept, her cheeks flushed, her heart beating unnaturally.

VII

Late that night.

She opened her eyes; she heard men's voices; she felt her heart still pounding within her at an alarming rate.

"And I told them then that it would come to no good end. Truly, the Lord does not countenance such joking."

She recognized the voices of Miles Standish and Elder Brewster.

"Well — what happened then?" This from Kennicott.

"Well, you see, Henry Haydock got some of this Mencken's medicine from one of the Indians. And he thought it would be a good joke to put it in the broth at the church supper this evening."

"Yes?"

"Well — he did it, the fool. And when the broth was served, hell on earth broke loose. Everyone started calling his neighbor a Puritan, and cursing him for having banished Beauty from the earth. The Lord knows what they meant by that; I don't. Old

20

friends fought like wildcats, shrieking 'Puritan!' at each other. Luckily it only got to one table — but there are ten raving lunatics in the lockup tonight.

"It's an awful thing. But thanks to the Lord, some good has come out of this evil: that medicine man, Mencken, was standing outside looking in at the rumpus, smiling to himself I guess. Well, somebody saw him and yelled, 'There's another of those damned Puritans!' and before he could get away five of them had jumped on him and beaten him to death. He deserved it, and it's a good joke on him that they killed him for being a Puritan."

Priscilla could stand no more. She rose from her bed, rushed into the room, and faced the three Puritans. In the voice of Priscilla Kennicott but with the words of the medicine man she scourged them.

"A good joke?" she began. "And that is what you Puritan gentlemen of God and volcanoes of Correct Thought snuffle over as a good joke? Well, with the highest respect to Professor Doctor Miles Standish, the Puritan Hearse-hound, and Professor Doctor Elder Brewster, the Plymouth Dr. Frank Crane — BLAA!"

She shrieked this last in their faces and fell lifeless at their feet.

She never recovered consciousness; an hour later she died. An overdose of the medicine had been too much for her weak heart.

"Poor William," comforted Elder Brewster, "you must be brave. You will miss her sorely. But console yourself with the thought that it was for the best. Priscilla has gone where she will always be happy. She has at last found that bliss which she searched for in vain on earth."

"Yes William," added Miles Standish. "Priscilla has now found eternal joy."

VIII

Heaven.

Smug saints with ill-fitting halos and imitation wings, singing meaningless hymns which Priscilla had heard countless times before.

Sleek prosaic angels flying aimlessly around playing stale songs on sickly yellow harps.

Three of the harps badly out of tune; two strings missing on another.

Moses, a Jew.

Methuselah, another Jew. Old and unshaven.

Priscilla threw herself on a cloud, sobbing.

"Well, sister, what seems to be the matter here?"

She looked up; she saw a sympathetic stranger looking down at her.

"Because you know, sister," he went on, "if you don't like it here you can always go back any time you want to."

"Do you mean to say," gasped Priscilla, "that I can return to earth?"

"You certainly can," said the stranger. "I'm sort of manager here, and whenever you see any particular part of the earth you'd like to live in, you just let me know and I'll arrange it."

He smiled and was gone.

IX

It was two hundred years before Priscilla Kennicott definitely decided that she could stand it no longer in heaven; it was another hundred years before she located a desirable place on earth to return to.

She finally selected a small town in the American northwest, far from the Puritan-tainted Plymouth; a small town in the midst of fields of beautiful waving grain; a small town free from the artificiality of large cities; a small town named Gopher Prairie.

She made known her desire to the manager; she said goodbye to a small group of friends who had gathered to see her off; she heard the sound of the eternal harp playing and hymn singing grow gradually fainter and fainter; she closed her eyes.

When she opened them again she found herself on Main Street in Gopher Prairie.

X

From the "Heavenly Harp and Trumpet":

Mrs. Priscilla Kennicott, one of our most popular angels, left these parts last Tuesday for an extended visit to the Earth. Mrs. K. confided to Ye Editor that she would probably take up her residence in Gopher Prairie, Minn., under the name of Carol Kennicott. The "Harp and Trumpet" felicitates the citizens of Gopher Prairie on their acquisition of a charming and up-to-date young matron whose absence will be keenly regretted by her

23

many friends in the heavenly younger married set. Good luck, Priscilla!

XI

Heaven.

Five years later.

The monthly meeting of the Celestial Browning Club.

Seated in the chair reserved for the guest of honor, the manager.

The meeting opens as usual with a reading by Brother Robert Browning of his poem "Pippa Passes;" as he proclaims that "God's in his heaven, all's right with the world," the members applaud and the manager rises and bows.

The chairman announces that "today we take up a subject in which I am sure we are all extremely interested — the popular literature of the United States."

The members listen to selected extracts from the writings of Gene Stratton-Porter, Zane Grey, and Harold Bell Wright; at the conclusion they applaud and the manager again bows.

"I am sure," says the chairman, "that we are all glad to hear that things are going so nicely in the United States." (Applause.) "And now, in conclusion, Brother Voltaire has requested permission to address us for a few minutes, and I am sure that anything Brother Voltaire has to say will be eminently worthwhile."

Brother Voltaire rises and announces that he has listened with interest to the discussion of American literature; that he, too, rejoices that all is well in this best of all possible United States;

24

and that he hopes they will pardon him if he supplements the program by reading a few extracts from another extremely popular American book recently published under the name of *Main Street.*

XII

At the next meeting of the Celestial Browning Club it was unanimously voted that the privileges of the club be denied Brother Voltaire for the period of one year, and that the name of Priscilla Kennicott be stricken from the list of non-resident members of heaven.

THE COURTSHIP OF MILES STANDISH

In the Manner of F. Scott Fitzgerald

This story occurs under the blue skies and bluer laws of Puritan New England, in the days when religion was still taken seriously by a great many people, and in the town of Plymouth where the "Mayflower," having ploughed its platitudinous way from Holland, had landed its precious cargo of pious Right Thinkers, moral Gentlemen of God, and – Priscilla.

Priscilla was – well, Priscilla had yellow hair. In a later generation, in a 1921 June, if she had toddled by at a country club dance you would have noticed first of all that glorious mass of bobbed corn-colored locks. You would, then, perhaps, have glanced idly at her face, and suddenly said "Oh my gosh!" The next moment you would have clutched the nearest stag and hissed, "Quick – yellow hair – silver dress – oh Judas!"

You would then have been introduced, and after dancing nine feet you would have been cut in on by another panting stag. In those nine delirious feet you would have become completely dazed by one of the smoothest lines since the building of the Southern Pacific. You would then have borrowed somebody's flask, gone into the locker room and gotten an edge – not a bachelor-dinner edge but just enough to give you the proper amount of confidence. You would have returned to the ballroom, cut in on this twentieth century Priscilla, and taken her and your edge out to a convenient limousine, or the first tee.

It was of some such yellow-haired Priscilla that Homer dreamed when he smote his lyre and chanted, "I sing of arms and the man;" it was at the sight of such as she that rare Ben Johnson's Dr. Faustus cried, "Was this the face that launched a thousand ships?" In all ages has such beauty enchanted the minds of men, calling forth in one century the Fiesolian terza rima of "Paradise Lost," in another the passionate arias of a dozen Beethoven symphonies. In 1620 the pagan daughter of Helen of Troy and Cleopatra of the Nile happened, by a characteristic jest of the great Ironist, to embark with her aunt on the "Mayflower."

Like all girls of eighteen Priscilla had learned to kiss and be kissed on every possible occasion; in the exotic and not at all uncommon pleasure of "petting" she had acquired infinite wisdom and complete disillusionment. But in all her "petting parties" on the "Mayflower" and in Plymouth she had found no Puritan who held her interest beyond the first kiss, and she had lately reverted in sheer boredom to her boarding school habit of drinking gin in large quantities, a habit which was not entirely approved of by her old-fashioned aunt, although Mrs. Brewster was glad to have her niece stay at home in the evenings "instead," as she told Mrs. Bradford, "of running around with those boys, and really, my dear, Priscilla says some of the FUNNIEST things when she gets a little, er – 'boiled,' as she calls it – you must come over some evening, and bring the governor."

Mrs. Brewster, Priscilla's aunt, is the ancestor of all New England aunts. She may be seen today walking down Tremont Street, Boston, in her Educator shoes on her way to S. S. Pierce's which she pronounces to rhyme with *hearse*. The twentieth century Mrs. Brewster wears a high-necked black silk waist with a chatelaine watch pinned over her left breast and a spot of Gordon's codfish (no bones) over her right. When

27

a little girl she was taken to see Longfellow, Lowell, and Ralph Waldo Emerson; she speaks familiarly of the James boys, but this has no reference to the well-known Missouri outlaws. She was brought up on blueberry cake, Postum and "The Atlantic Monthly;" she loves the Boston "Transcript," God, and her relatives in Newton Centre. Her idea of a daring joke is the remark Susan Hale made to Edward Everett Hale about sending underwear to the heathen. She once asked Donald Ogden Stewart to dinner with her niece; she didn't think his story about the lady mind reader who read the man's mind and then slapped his face, was very funny; she never asked him again.

The action of this story all takes place in MRS. BREWSTER'S Plymouth home on two successive June evenings. As the figurative curtain rises MRS. BREWSTER is sitting at a desk reading the latest installment of Foxe's "Book of Martyrs."

The sound of a clanking sword is heard outside. MRS. BREWSTER looks up, smiles to herself, and goes on reading. A knock – a timid knock.

MRS. BREWSTER: Come in.

(Enter CAPTAIN MILES STANDISH, whiskered and forty. In a later generation, with that imposing mustache and his hatred of Indians, Miles would undoubtedly have been a bank president. At present he seems somewhat ill at ease, and obviously relieved to find only PRISCILLA'S aunt at home.)

MRS. BREWSTER: Good evening, Captain Standish.

MILES: Good evening, Mrs. Brewster. It's – it's cool for June, isn't it?

MRS. BREWSTER: Yes. I suppose we'll pay, for it with a hot July, though.

MILES (nervously): Yes, but it – it is cool for June, isn't it?

MRS. BREWSTER: So you said, Captain.

MILES: Yes. So I said, didn't I? (Silence.)

MILES: Mistress Priscilla isn't home, then?

MRS. BREWSTER: Why, I don't think so, Captain But I never can be sure where Priscilla is.

MILES (eagerly): She's a – a fine girl, isn't she? A fine girl.

MRS. BREWSTER: Why, yes. Of course, Priscilla has her faults but she'd make some man a fine wife – some man who knew how to handle her – an older man, with experience.

MILES: Do you really think so, Mrs. Brewster? (After a minute.) Do you think Priscilla is thinking about marrying anybody in particular?

MRS. BREWSTER: Well, I can't say, Captain. You know – she's a little wild. Her mother was wild, too, you know – that is, before the Lord spoke to her. They say she used to be seen at the Mermaid Tavern in London with all those play-acting people. She always used to say that Priscilla would marry a military man.

MILES: A military man? Well, now tell me Mrs. Brewster, do you think that a sweet delicate creature like Priscilla –

A VOICE (in the next room): Oh DAMN!

MRS. BREWSTER: That must be Priscilla now.

THE VOICE: Auntie!

MRS. BREWSTER: Yes, Priscilla dear.

THE VOICE: Where in hell did you put the vermouth?

MRS. BREWSTER: In the cupboard, dear. I do hope you aren't going to get – er – "boiled" again tonight, Priscilla.

(Enter PRISCILLA, infinitely radiant, infinitely beautiful, with a bottle of vermouth in one hand and a jug of gin in the other.)

PRISCILLA: Auntie, that was a dirty trick to hide the vermouth. Hello Miles – shoot many Indians today?

MILES: Why – er – no, Mistress Priscilla.

PRISCILLA: Wish you'd take me with you next time, Miles. I'd love to shoot an Indian, wouldn't you, auntie?

MRS. BREWSTER: Priscilla! What an idea! And please dear, give Auntie Brewster the gin. I – er – promised to take some to the church social tonight and it's almost all gone now.

MILES: I didn't see you at church last night, Mistress Priscilla.

PRISCILLA: Well I'll tell you, Miles. I started to go to church – really felt awfully religious. But just as I was leaving I thought, "Priscilla, how about a drink – just one little drink?" You know, Miles, church goes so much better when you're just a little boiled – the lights and everything just kind of – oh, its glorious. Well last night, after I'd had a little liquor, the funniest thing happened. I felt awfully good, not like church at all – so I just thought I'd take a walk in the woods. And I came to a pool – a wonderful honest-to-God pool – with the moon shining right into the middle of it. So I just undressed and dove in and it was the most marvelous thing in the world. And then I danced on the bank in the grass and the moonlight – oh, Lordy, Miles, you ought to have seen me.

MRS. BREWSTER: Priscilla!

PRISCILLA: 'Scuse me, Auntie Brewster. And then I just lay in the grass and sang and laughed.

MRS. BREWSTER: Dear, you'll catch your death of cold one of these nights. I hope you'll excuse me, Captain Standish; it's time I was going to our social. I'll leave Priscilla to entertain you. Now be a good girl, Priscilla, and please dear don't drink straight vermouth – remember what happened last time. Good night, Captain – good night, dear.

(Exit MRS. BREWSTER with gin.)

PRISCILLA: Oh damn! What'll we do, Miles – I'm getting awfully sleepy.

MILES: Why – we might – er – pet a bit.

PRISCILLA (yawning): No. I'm too tired – besides, I hate whiskers.

MILES: Yes, that's so, I remember.

(Ten minutes' silence, with MILES looking sentimentally into the fireplace, PRISCILLA curled up in a chair on the other side.)

MILES: I was – your aunt and I – we were talking about you before you came in. It was a talk that meant a lot to me.

PRISCILLA: Miles, would you mind closing that window?

(MILES closes the window and returns to his chair by the fireplace.)

MILES: And your aunt told me that your mother said you would some day marry a military man.

PRISCILLA: Miles, would you mind passing me that pillow over there?

(MILES gets up, takes the pillow to PRISCILLA and again sits down.)

MILES: And I thought that if you wanted a military man, why – well, I've always thought a great deal of you, Mistress Priscilla – and since my Rose died I've been pretty lonely, and while I'm nothing but a rough old soldier yet – well, what I'm driving at is – you see, maybe you and I could sort of – well, I'm not much of a hand at fancy love speeches and all that – but –

(He is interrupted by a snore. He glances up and sees that PRISCILLA has fallen fast asleep. He sits looking hopelessly into the fireplace for a long time, then gets up, puts on his hat and tiptoes out of the door.)

THE NEXT EVENING

PRISCILLA is sitting alone, lost in reverie, before the fireplace. It is almost as if she had not moved since the evening before.

A knock, and the door opens to admit JOHN ALDEN, nonchalant, disillusioned, and twenty-one.

JOHN: Good evening. Hope I don't bother you.

PRISCILLA: The only people who bother me are women who tell me I'm beautiful and men who don't.

JOHN: Not a very brilliant epigram – but still – yes, you ARE beautiful.

PRISCILLA: Of course, if it's an effort for you to say –

JOHN: Nothing is worthwhile without effort.

PRISCILLA: Sounds like Miles Standish; many things I do without effort are worthwhile; I am beautiful without the slightest effort.

JOHN: Yes, you're right. I could kiss you without any effort – and that would be worthwhile – perhaps.

PRISCILLA: Kissing me would prove nothing. I kiss as casually as I breathe.

JOHN: And if you didn't breathe – or kiss – you would die.

PRISCILLA: Any woman would.

JOHN: Then you are like other women. How unfortunate.

PRISCILLA: I am like no woman you ever knew.

JOHN: You arouse my curiosity.

PRISCILLA: Curiosity killed a cat.

JOHN: A cat may look at a – Queen.

PRISCILLA: And a Queen keeps cats for her amusement. They purr so delightfully when she pets them.

JOHN: I never learned to purr; it must be amusing – for the Queen.

PRISCILLA: Let me teach you. I'm starting a new class tonight.

JOHN: I'm afraid I couldn't afford to pay the tuition.

PRISCILLA: For a few exceptionally meritorious pupils, various scholarships and fellowships have been provided.

JOHN: By whom? Old graduates?

PRISCILLA: No – the institution has been endowed by God –

JOHN: With exceptional beauty – I'm afraid I'm going to kiss you. Now.

(They kiss.)

(Ten minutes pass.)

PRISCILLA: Stop smiling in that inane way.

JOHN: I just happened to think of something awfully funny. You know the reason why I came over here tonight?

PRISCILLA: To see me. I wondered why you hadn't come months ago.

JOHN: No. It's really awfully funny – but I came here tonight because Miles Standish made me promise this morning to ask you to marry him. Miles is an awfully good egg, really Priscilla.

PRISCILLA: Speak for yourself, John. (They kiss.)

PRISCILLA: Again.

JOHN: Again – and again. Oh Lord, I'm gone.

(An hour later JOHN leaves. As the door closes behind him PRISCILLA sinks back into her chair before the fireplace; an hour passes, and she does not move; her aunt returns from the Bradfords' and after a few ineffectual attempts at conversation goes to bed alone; the candles gutter, flicker, and die out; the room is filled of sacred silence. Once more the clock chimes forth the hour – the hour of fluted peace, of dead desire and epic love. Oh not for aye, Endymion, mayst thou unfold the purple panoply of priceless years. She sleeps – PRISCILLA sleeps – and down the palimpsest of age-old passion the lyres of night breathe forth their poignant praise. She sleeps – eternal Helen – in the moonlight of a thousand years; immortal symbol of immortal aeons, flower of the gods transplanted on a foreign shore, infinitely rare, infinitely erotic. [1])

[1] For the further adventures of Priscilla, see F. Scott Fitzgerald's stories in the "Girl With the Yellow Hair" series, notably "This Side of Paradise," "The Offshore Pirate," "The Ice Palace," "Head and Shoulders," "Bernice Bobs Her Hair," "Benediction" and "The Beautiful and Damned."

Robert Benchley

1889–1945

"I'm not a writer...I'm not an actor. I don't know what I am."

"Robert Charles Benchley, born on the Isle of Wight, September 15, 1807. Shipped as a cabin boy on the Florence J. Marble, 1815. Arrested for bigamy and murder in Port Said, 1817. Released, 1820. Wrote Tale of Two Cities. Married Princess Anastasia of Portugal, 1831. Children: Prince Rupprecht and several little girls. Wrote Uncle Tom's Cabin, 1850. Editor of Godey's Ladies Book, 1851-1856. Began Les Misérables in 1870, finished by Victor Hugo. Died 1871. Buried in Westminster Abbey."

So wrote Robert Benchley of his own life. While his true biography may not have been as fantastical as he imagined, it was no less prolific and was filled with its own brand of humor and drama.

Robert Benchley was actually born in Worcester, Massachusetts to Charles and Maria Jane Moran ("Jennie") Benchley. His older brother, Edmund, who was thirteen years his senior, attended West Point and fought in Cuba during the Spanish-American War. When Robert was very young, tragedy befell the family. A news reporter visited his mother to inform her that Edmund had been killed in the war. Upon receiving the news, his mother blurted out, "Why couldn't it have been Robert?!" – A comment she would regret and would attempt many times in her life to make up for. Fiancée of the late Edmund, Lillian Duryea, who was fortunate enough to come from family money, turned her attention to Robert during this traumatic time and decided to help him out of Worcester and into school.

With the aid of Duryea's finances, Benchley enrolled in Harvard University in 1908. In addition to acting in several productions put on by the Hasty Pudding Theatricals, he worked with the *Harvard Lampoon*, where he was elected to the board of directors in his third year. It was with his participation in these extracurricular activities that Benchley's humor and style began to emerge, often to his academic detriment. During his senior year, he was assigned to write a final paper discussing the U.S.–Canadian Fisheries Dispute. He began: "I know nothing about the point of view of Great Britain in the arbitration of the international fishing problem, and nothing about the point of view of the United States. Therefore I shall discuss the question from the point of view of the fish." Benchley was not awarded a degree until he rewrote his composition.

Following Harvard, Benchley embarked on a series of short-lived jobs, including a stint in advertising as well as translating French catalogues for the Boston Museum of Fine Arts. Eventually, he found a position with the *New York Tribune* as a reporter, albeit not a very good one, as he even admitted. When the *Tribune*'s Sunday magazine was launched, however, Benchley was moved to their staff, soon becoming chief writer. He wrote two articles per week, one of which was a feature-style article on whatever topic he wished. Although his pieces were very popular with readers, Benchley's pacifist stance over the U.S.'s involvement in The Great War was not popular with management at the *Tribune*. When the magazine folded in 1917, he found himself out of work.

During this time, Benchley had been submitting freelance articles to *Vanity Fair* with uneven success. Sometime after his work with the *Tribune* ended, he was offered an associate editor position with *Collier's* magazine. Sensing *Vanity Fair* would be a better match for him, he took the *Collier's* offer to the competing magazine to see if they would counter it with an offer of their own. The gamble worked, and Benchley signed on as managing editor of *Vanity Fair* in 1919.

It was at *Vanity Fair* that Benchley met and worked with Robert E. Sherwood and Dorothy Parker, and the seeds of the Algonquin Round Table were planted. The trio became fast friends. They were also inseparable cohorts in office antics, much to the consternation of management at *Vanity Fair*. When their employer demanded that all employees submit tardy slips in any instance of lateness, Benchley, in very small handwriting, filled a slip with a highly detailed account of his having to wrangle escaped elephants from the Hippodrome, thus his tardiness of 11 minutes. He was not issued a tardy slip again.

Eventually, the trio's rebelliousness at *Vanity Fair* caught up with them. Dorothy Parker was fired, ostensibly because of overly-vicious theatrical reviews. In what Parker called "the greatest act of friendship I'd ever seen," Benchley and Sherwood tendered their resignations in solidarity. Once again unemployed, this time married with two children to raise, Benchley decided to free-lance. He and Parker rented an office so small, Benchley indicated that if it was one cubic foot less in space, it "would have constituted adultery."

In the early 1920s, Robert Benchley's career began to take off. In addition to writing a weekly book review column

39

for *New York World*, he was regularly submitting humor columns to several publications, including *The New Yorker* and *Life*. The notoriety of the Algonquin Round Table was also growing. Their theater production *No Sirree!* featured a Benchley skit called "The Treasurer's Report," in which he played an assistant treasurer failing miserably at summarizing his club's yearly expenses. *No Sirree!* was a hit, with "The Treasurer's Report" garnering a great deal of the attention – so much so, the fledgling film community took notice. Fox Films invited Benchley to make a talking film version of his skit, which he heartily accepted. Filmed in Astoria, Queens, in New York City, the short film was met with critical and financial success upon its release in 1928. Two other films, *The Sex Life of the Polyp*, in which he wrote and starred, and *Spellbinder*, in which he starred, were met with similar accolades. During this time, Benchley continued writing for *The New Yorker*, with the magazine publishing an average of 48 of his columns per year. Fellow Round Table members Alexander Woollcott and Dorothy Parker were also regular contributors to the magazine, and the publication flourished.

Even with his success in the literary world, the lure of filmmaking continued to beckon Benchley. RKO Pictures offered him writing and acting contracts for more money than he was making at *The New Yorker*, and at the height of the Great Depression, Benchley devoted a large part of his time to film-making. In addition to his contracts with RKO, Benchley completed short films and features for both Universal Pictures and Metro-Goldwyn-Mayer, including a parody of the Mellon Institute's study on sleep. The short film, entitled *How to Sleep*, featured Benchley as both the narrator and sleeper, and became the work for which he was best known, earning an Academy Award for Best Short Subject in 1935.

Throughout the 1930s, Benchley continued to make movies at an almost dizzying pace, as well as writing three syndicated magazine columns simultaneously. He had garnered a contract that allowed him to produce short films in New York, and Benchley found himself sometimes completing two shoots a day. The sheer volume of creative output gave Benchley a very large public profile, and he was offered his own radio show as well as numerous appearances on television.

Benchley's wild success took a downturn in 1939, however. His radio show was not as well received as he had hoped it would be, and after a three-year run, was cancelled. He learned that MGM was not going to renew his contract, and *The New Yorker*, frustrated over the precedence that his film career had taken over his work at the magazine, hired someone else to take his place. Benchley continued to make films for Paramount, but these were not met with nearly the success of his previous works. By the 1940s, he had been reduced to taking roles in the film company's least distinguished pictures.

While publication of his collected writings and his work in the movies kept him financially solvent, Benchley was not happy with the turn his career had taken. The man who had been an ardent teetotaler in his youth had developed a drinking problem. In the mid-1940s, his alcoholism had worsened to the point that he was diagnosed with cirrhosis of the liver, and his health continued to deteriorate even as he continued to work. Robert Benchley died at age 56 in a New York hospital on November 21, 1945. Despite what seems to be a rather sorrowful denouement to his life, Robert Benchley left behind an amazingly bountiful legacy of humor and wit that continues to endure.

RULES AND SUGGESTIONS FOR WATCHING AUCTION BRIDGE

With all the expert advice that is being offered in print these days about how to play games, it seems odd that no one has formulated a set of rules for the spectators. The spectators are much more numerous than the players, and seem to need more regulation. As a spectator of twenty years standing, versed in watching all sports except six-day bicycle races, I offer the fruit of my experience in the form of suggestions and reminiscences which may tend to clarify the situation, or, in case there is no situation which needs clarifying, to make one.

In the event of a favorable reaction on the part of the public, I shall form an association, to be known as the National Amateur Audience Association (or the N.A.A.A., if you are given to slang) of which I shall be Treasurer. That's all I ask, the Treasurership.

This being an off-season of the year for outdoor sports (except walking, which is getting to have neither participants nor spectators) it seems best to start with a few remarks on the strenuous occupation of watching a bridge game. Bridge-watchers are not so numerous as football watchers, for instance, but they are much more in need of coordination and it will be the aim of this article to formulate a standardized set of rules for watching bridge which may be taken as a criterion for the whole country.

NUMBER WHO MAY WATCH

There should not be more than one watcher for each table. When there are two, or more, confusion is apt to result and no one of the watchers can devote his attention to the game as it should be devoted. Two watchers are also likely to bump into each other as they make their way around the table looking over the players' shoulders. If there are more watchers than there are tables, two can share one table between them, one being dummy while the other watches. In this event the first one should watch until the hand has been dealt and six tricks taken, being relieved by the second one for the remaining tricks and the marking down of the score.

PRELIMINARIES

In order to avoid any charge of signaling, it will be well for the following conversational formula to be used before the game begins:

The ring-leader of the game says to the fifth person: "Won't you join the game and make a fourth? I have some work which I really ought to be doing."

The fifth person replies: "Oh, no, thank you! I play a wretched game. I'd much rather sit here and read, if you don't mind."

To which the ring-leader replies: "Pray do."

After the first hand has been dealt, the fifth person, whom we shall now call the "watcher," puts down the book and leans forward in his (or her) chair, craning the neck to see what is in the hand nearest him. The strain becoming too great, he arises and approaches the table, saying: "Do you mind if I watch a bit?"

No answer need be given to this, unless someone at the table has nerve enough to tell the truth.

PROCEDURE

The game is now on. The watcher walks around the table, giving each hand a careful scrutiny, groaning slightly at the sight of a poor one and making noises of joyful anticipation at the good ones. Stopping behind an especially unpromising array of cards, it is well to say: "Well, unlucky at cards, lucky in love, you know." This gives the partner an opportunity to judge his chances on the bid he is about to make, and is perfectly fair to the other side, too, for they are not left entirely in the dark. Thus everyone benefits by the remark.

When the bidding begins, the watcher has considerable opportunity for effective work. Having seen how the cards lie, he is able to stand back and listen with a knowing expression, laughing at unjustified bids and urging on those who should, in his estimation, plunge. At the conclusion of the bidding he should say: "Well, we're off!"

As the hand progresses and the players become intent on the game, the watcher may be the cause of no little innocent diversion. He may ask one of the players for a match, or, standing behind the one who is playing the hand, he may say:

"I'll give you three guesses as to whom I ran into on the street yesterday. Someone you all know. Used to go to school with you, Harry... light hair and blue eyes... medium build... well, sir, it was Lew Milliken. Yessir, Lew Milliken. Hadn't seen him for fifteen years. Asked after you, Harry... and George too. And what do you think he told me about Chick?"

Answers may or may not be returned to these remarks, according to the good nature of the players, but in any event, they serve their purpose of distraction.

Particular care should be taken that no one of the players is allowed to make a mistake. The watcher, having his mind free, is naturally in a better position to keep track of matters of sequence and revoking. Thus, he may say:

"The lead was over here, George," or

"I think that you refused spades a few hands ago, Lillian."

Of course, there are some watchers who have an inherited delicacy about offering advice or talking to the players. Some people are that way. They are interested in the game, and love to watch but they feel that they ought not to interfere. I had a cousin who just wouldn't talk while a hand was being played, and so, as she had to do something, she hummed. She didn't hum very well, and her program was limited to the first two lines of "How Firm a Foundation," but she carried it off very well and often got the players to humming it along with her. She could also drum rather well with her fingers on the back of the chair of one of the players while looking over his shoulder. "How Firm a Foundation" didn't lend itself very well to drumming; so she had a little patrol that she worked up all by herself, beginning soft, like a drum corps in the distance, and getting louder and louder, finally dying away again so that you could barely near it. It was wonderful how she could do it — and still go on living.

Those who feel this way about talking while others are playing bridge have a great advantage over my cousin and her class if they can play the piano. They play ever so softly, in

45

order not to disturb, but somehow or other you just know that they are there, and that the next to last note in the coda is going to be very sour.

But, of course, the piano work does not technically come under the head of watching, although when there are two watchers to a table, one may go over to the piano while she is dummy.

But your real watcher will allow nothing to interfere with his conscientious following of the game, and it is for real watchers only that these suggestions have been formulated. The minute you get out of the class of those who have the best interests of the game at heart, you become involved in dilettantism and amateurishness, and the whole sport of bridge-watching falls into disrepute.

The only trouble with the game as it now stands is the risk of personal injury. This can be eliminated by the watcher insisting on each player being frisked for weapons before the game begins and cultivating a good serviceable defense against ordinary forms of fistic attack.

HOW TO WATCH A CHESS MATCH

Second in the list of games which it is necessary for every sportsman to know how to watch comes chess. If you don't know how to watch chess, the chances are that you will never have any connection with the game whatsoever. You would not, by any chance, be playing it yourself.

I know some very nice people that play chess, mind you, and I wouldn't have thought that I was in any way spoofing at the game. I would sooner spoof at the people who engineered the Panama Canal or who are drawing up plans for the vehicular tunnel under the Hudson River. I am no man to make light of chess and its adherents, although they might very well make light of me. In fact, they have.

But what I say is, that taking society by and large, man and boy, the chances are that chess would be the Farmer-Labor Party among the contestants for sporting honors.

Now, since it is settled that you probably will not want to play chess, unless you should be laid up with a bad knee-pain or something, it follows that, if you want to know anything about the sport at all, you will have to watch it from the side-lines. That is what this series of lessons aims to teach you to do (of course, if you are going to be nasty and say that you don't want even to watch it, why all this time has been wasted on my part as well as on yours).

HOW TO FIND A GAME TO WATCH

The first problem confronting the chess spectator is to find some people who are playing. The bigger the city, the

47

harder it is to find anyone indulging in chess. In a small town you can usually go straight to Wilbur Tatnuck's General Store, and be fairly sure of finding a quiet game in progress over behind the stove and the crate of pilot-biscuit, but as you draw away from the mitten district you find the sporting instinct of the population cropping out in other lines and chess becoming more and more restricted to the sheltered corners of Y.M.C.A. club-rooms and exclusive social organizations.

However, we shall have to suppose, in order to get any article written at all, that you have found two people playing chess somewhere. They probably will neither see nor hear you as you come up on them so you can stand directly behind the one who is defending the south goal without fear of detection.

THE DETAILS OF THE GAME

At first you may think that they are both dead, but a mirror held to the lips of the nearest contestant will probably show moisture (unless, of course, they really should be dead, which would be a horrible ending for a little lark like this. I once heard of a murderer who propped his two victims up against a chess board in sporting attitudes and was able to get as far as Seattle before his crime was discovered).

Soon you will observe a slight twitching of an eyelid or a moistening of the lips and then, like a greatly retarded moving-picture of a person passing the salt, one of the players will lift a chess-man from one spot on the board and place it on another spot.

It would be best not to stand too close to the board at this time as you are likely to be trampled on in the excitement.

48

For this action that you have just witnessed corresponds to a run around right end in a football game or a two-bagger in baseball, and is likely to cause considerable enthusiasm on the one hand and deep depression on the other. They may even forget themselves to the point of shifting their feet or changing the hands on which they are resting their foreheads. Almost anything is liable to happen.

When the commotion has died down a little, it will be safe for you to walk around and stand behind the other player and wait there for the next move. While waiting it would be best to stand with the weight of your body evenly distributed between your two feet, for you will probably be standing there a long time and if you bear down on one foot all of the time, that foot is bound to get tired. A comfortable stance for watching chess is with the feet slightly apart (perhaps a foot or a foot and a half), with a slight bend at the knees to rest the legs and the weight of the body thrown forward on the balls of the feet. A rhythmic rising on the toes, holding the hands behind the back, the head well up and the chest out, introduces a note of variety into the position which will be welcome along about dusk.

Not knowing anything about the game, you will perhaps find it difficult at first to keep your attention on the board. This can be accomplished by means of several little optical tricks. For instance, if you look at the black and white squares on the board very hard and for a very long time, they will appear to jump about and change places. The black squares will rise from the board about a quarter of an inch and slightly overlap the white ones. Then, if you change focus suddenly, the white squares will do the same thing to the black ones. And finally, after doing this until someone asks you what you are looking cross-eyed for, if you will shut your eyes tight you will see an exact reproduction of the chess board, done in pink and green, in your mind's eye. By this time, the players will be almost ready for another move.

This will make two moves that you have watched. It is now time to get a little fancy work into your game. About an hour will have already gone by and you should be so thoroughly grounded in the fundamentals of chess watching that you can proceed to the next step.

Have some one of your friends bring you a chair, a table and an old pyrography outfit, together with some book-ends on which to burn a design.

Seat yourself at the table in the chair and (if I remember the process correctly) squeeze the bulb attached to the needle until the latter becomes red hot. Then, grasping the book-ends in the left hand, carefully trace around the penciled design with the point of the needle. It probably will be a picture of the Lion of Lucerne, and you will let the needle slip on the way round the face, giving it the appearance of having shaved in a Pullman that morning. But that really won't make any difference, for the whole thing is not so much to do a nice pair of book-ends as to help you along in watching the chess match.

If you have any scruples against burning wood, you may knit something, or paste stamps in an album.

And before you know it, the game will be over and you can put on your things and go home.

Bon Bons, Bourbon and Bon Mots

HOW TO BE A SPECTATOR AT SPRING PLANTING

The danger in watching gardening, as in watching many other sports, is that you may be drawn into it yourself. This you must fight against. Your sinecure standing depends on a rigid abstinence from any of the work itself. Once you stoop over to hold one end of a string for a groaning planter, once you lift one shovelful of earth or toss out one stone, you become a worker and a worker is an abomination in the eyes of the true garden watcher.

A fence is, therefore, a great help. You may take up your position on the other side of the fence from the garden and lean heavily against it smoking a pipe, or you may even sit on it. Anything so long as you are out of helping distance and yet near enough so that the worker will be within easy range of your voice. You ought to be able to point a great deal, also.

There is much to be watched during the early stages of garden preparation. Nothing is so satisfying as to lean ruminatingly against a fence and observe the slow, rhythmic swing of the digger's back or hear the repeated scraping of the shovel-edge against some buried rock. It sometimes is a help to the digger to sing a chant, just to give him the beat. And then sometimes it is not. He will tell you in case he doesn't need it.

There is always a great deal for the watcher to do in the nature of comment on the soil. This is especially true if it is a new garden or has never been cultivated before by the present owner. The idea is to keep the owner from becoming too sanguine over the prospects.

"That soil looks pretty clayey," is a good thing to say. (It is hard to say clearly, too. You had better practice it before trying it out on the gardener.)

"I don't think that you'll have much luck with potatoes in that kind of earth," is another helpful approach. It is even better to go at it the other way, finding out first what the owner expects to plant. It may be that he isn't going to plant any potatoes, and then there you are, stuck with a perfectly dandy prediction which has no bearing on the case. It is time enough to pull it after he has told you that he expects to plant peas, beans, beets, corn. Then you can interrupt him and say: "Corn?" incredulously. "You don't expect to get any corn in that soil do you? Don't you know that corn requires a large percentage of bi-carbonate of soda in the soil, and I don't think, from the looks that there is an ounce of soda bi-carb in your whole plot. Even if the corn does come up, it will be so tough you can't eat it."

Then you can laugh, and call out to a neighbor, or even to the man's wife: "Hey, what do you know? Steve here thinks he's going to get some corn up in this soil!"

The watcher will find plenty to do when the time comes to pick the stones out of the freshly turned-over earth. It is his work to get upon a high place where he can survey the whole garden and detect the more obvious rocks.

"Here is a big fella over here, Steve," he may say. Or: "Just run your rake a little over in that corner. I'll bet you'll find a nest of them there."

"Plymouth Rock" is a funny thing to call any particularly offensive boulder, and is sure to get a laugh, especially if you kid the digger good-naturedly about being a Pilgrim and landing on it. He may even give it to you to keep.

Just as a matter of convenience for the worker, watchers have sometimes gone to the trouble of keeping count of the number of stones thrown out. This is done by shouting out the count after each stone has been tossed. It makes a sort of game of the thing, and in this spirit the digger may be urged on to make a record.

"That's forty-eight, old man! Come on now, make her fifty. Attaboy, forty-nine! Only one more to go. We-want-fifty-we-want-fifty-we-want-fifty!"

And not only stones will be found, but queer objects which have got themselves buried in the ground during the winter months and have become metamorphosed, so they are half way between one thing and another. As the digger holds one of these *objets dirt* gingerly between his thumb and forefinger the watcher has plenty of opportunity to shout out:

"You'd better save that. It may come in handy some day. What is it, Eddie? Your old beard?"

And funny cracks like that.

Here is where it is going to be difficult to keep to your resolution about not helping. After the digging, and stoning, and turning-over has been done, and the ground is all nice and soft and loamy, the idea of running a rake softly over the susceptible surface and leaving a beautiful even design in its wake, is almost too tempting to be withstood.

The worker himself will do all that he can to make it hard for you. He will rake with evident delight, much longer

53

than is necessary, back and forth, across and back, cocking his head and surveying the pattern and fixing it up along the edges with a care which is nothing short of insulting considering the fact that the whole thing has got to be mussed up again when the planting begins.

If you feel that you can no longer stand it without offering to assist, get down from the fence and go into your own house and up to your own room. There pray for strength. By the time you come down, the owner of the garden ought to have stopped raking and got started on the planting.

Here the watcher's task is almost entirely advisory. And, for the first part of the planting, he should lie low and say nothing. Wait until the planter has got his rows marked out and has wobbled along on his knees pressing the seeds into perhaps half the length of his first row. Then say:

"Hey there, Charlie! You've got those rows going the wrong way."

Charlie will say no he hasn't. Then he will ask what you mean the wrong way.

"Why, you poor sod, you've got them running north and south. They ought to go east and west. The sun rises over there, doesn't it?" (Charlie will attempt to deny this, but you must go right on.) "And it comes on up behind that tree and over my roof and sets over there, doesn't it?" (By this time, Charlie will be crying with rage.) "Well, just as soon as your beans get up an inch or two they are going to cast a shadow right down the whole row and only those in front will ever get any sun. You can't grow things without sun, you know."

If Charlie takes you seriously and starts in to rearrange his rows in the other direction, you might perhaps get down off the fence and go in the house. You have done enough. If he doesn't take you seriously, you surely had better go in.

HOW TO UNDERSTAND INTERNATIONAL FINANCE

It is high time that someone came out with a clear statement of the international financial situation. For weeks and weeks officials have been rushing about holding conferences and councils and having their pictures taken going up and down the steps of buildings. Then, after each conference, the newspapers have printed a lot of figures showing the latest returns on how much Germany owes the bank. And none of it means anything.

Now there is a certain principle which has to be followed in all financial discussions involving sums over one hundred dollars. There is probably not more than one hundred dollars in actual cash in circulation today. That is, if you were to call in all the bills and silver and gold in the country at noon tomorrow and pile them up on the table, you would find that you had just about one hundred dollars, with perhaps several Canadian pennies and a few peppermint life-savers. All the rest of the money you hear about doesn't exist. It is conversation-money. When you hear of a transaction involving $50,000,000, it means that one firm wrote "50,000,000" on a piece of paper and gave it to another firm, and the other firm took it home and said "Look, Momma, I got $50,000,000!" But when Momma asked for a dollar and a quarter out of it to pay the man who washed the windows, the answer probably was that the firm hadn't got more than seventy cents in cash.

This is the principle of finance. So long as you can pronounce any number above a thousand, you have got that much money. You can't work this scheme with the shoe-store man or the restaurant-owner, but it goes big on Wall Street or in international financial circles.

56

This much understood, we see that when the Allies demand 132,000,000,000 gold marks from Germany they know very well that nobody in Germany has ever seen 132,000,000,000 gold marks and never will. A more surprised and disappointed lot of boys you couldn't ask to see than the Supreme Financial Council would be if Germany were actually to send them a money-order for the full amount demanded.

What they mean is that, taken all in all, Germany owes the world 132,000,000,000 gold marks plus carfare. This includes everything, breakage, meals sent to room, good will, everything. Now, it is understood that if they really meant this, Germany couldn't even draw cards; so the principle on which the thing is figured out is as follows: (Watch this closely; there is a trick in it).

You put down a lot of figures, like this. Any figures will do, so long as you can't read them quickly:

132,000,000,000 gold marks

$33,000,000,000 on a current value basis

$21,000,000,000 on reparation account plus 12-1/2% yearly tax on German exports

11,000,000,000 gold fish

$1.35 amusement tax

866,000 miles

Diameter of the sun

57

2,000,000,000

27,000,000,000

31,000,000,000

 Then you add them together and subtract the number you first thought of. This leaves 11. And the card you hold in your hand is the seven of diamonds. Am I right?

Dorothy Parker

1893–1967

"I might repeat to myself slowly and soothingly, a list of quotations beautiful from minds profound – if I can remember any of the damn things."

Dorothy Parker was born Dorothy Rothschild to Jacob and Eliza Rothschild on August 22 in Long Branch, New Jersey. Her parents were middle-class residents of Manhattan who had a summer cottage in the small seaside town, some 60 miles south of New York City. While Parker was always considered a New Yorker, she would be the first one to wryly point out her birthplace, writing once, "I was cheated out of the distinction of being a native New Yorker, because I had to go and get born while the family was spending the summer in New Jersey, but honestly, we came back into town right after Labor Day, so I nearly made the grade."

Just before Parker's fifth birthday, her mother died. Her father remarried in 1900 to Eleanor Lewis, with whom Parker did not get along, and to whom she referred as "the housekeeper." Even though her father was Jewish, Parker attended Roman Catholic elementary school followed by finishing school in Morristown, New Jersey. Parker's formal education ended at age 13. A few years later, her father died, and Parker moved back to New York to write verse during the day while earning money at night playing piano at a school for dance.

In 1914, Parker sold her first poem to *Vanity Fair*. Two years later, the editor of *Vogue* not only bought some of her poetry, but also offered her an editorial position on the magazine. Parker worked at *Vogue* for two years, then moved to *Vanity Fair* as a staff writer. In 1917, she met and married stockbroker Edwin Pond Parker II. The marriage lasted 11 years, but was largely an unhappy one, as the two were separated by his service in World War I. Edwin Parker was wounded in the war, and an already burgeoning alcohol problem was made worse by his becoming addicted to morphine that was first administered to him during his military service.

In 1918, Parker began writing theater criticism for *Vanity Fair* as a stand-in for the vacationing P.G. Wodehouse, and her career began to take off. Here she met Robert Benchley and Robert E. Sherwood, and the trio began to have lunches together at the Algonquin Hotel. The group started to expand, and soon became the infamous Algonquin Round Table. Newspaper columnist Franklin Pierce Adams would often reprint Parker's lunchtime remarks and short verse in his widely read "The Conning Tower," giving her national exposure.

Despite her growing popularity, Parker's caustic wit eventually caused her termination from *Vanity Fair*. Editors at the magazine worried that too many influential producers were becoming offended by Parker's biting remarks, so she was fired. Benchley and Sherwood, in an act of friendship, resigned in solidarity with her. Parker and Benchley found work soon after in 1925 as part of the "board of editors" of Harold Ross' new venture *The New Yorker*, however, and Parker began a 15 year stretch of unmatched success.

In addition to her poems being published in *Vogue*, *Vanity Fair*, and *The New Yorker* throughout the 1920s, Parker also contributed to *Life*, *McCall's*, and *The New Republic*. Her first volume of collected poetry, *Enough Rope*, was published in 1926. The book was a popular and critical success, selling 47,000 copies and cementing her reputation as the literary world's top sardonic wit. She followed *Enough Rope* with more volumes of verse, *Sunset Gun* (1928) and *Death and Taxes* (1931), as well as the short story collections *Laments for the Living* (1930) and *After Such Pleasures* (1933). *The New Yorker* was also home to Parker's popular "Constant Reader" book review column that ran from 1927 to 1933. In 1929, Parker was awarded the O. Henry Award for best short story for "Big Blonde," originally published in *The Bookman* magazine.

During this time when Parker's literary career was most prolific and successful, her personal life seemed to be less than ideal. She began to drink heavily. In the 1920s, she and Edwin Parker had separated, and Dorothy Parker had several extra-marital affairs, including one with emerging playwright Charles MacArthur. Parker became pregnant with MacArthur's child, and subsequently had an abortion. It was shortly after that Parker first attempted suicide by slitting her wrists. The pattern of depression, suicide attempts, and recovery would become a constant in Parker's life, though professionally she would maintain a steady work ethic. Never one to shy away from uncomfortable topics, Parker would even incorporate the themes of suicide, alcohol and failed love affairs (always with an acerbic flair) into her writing.

Starting in the 1930s, Parker began writing for the stage and screen. She collaborated on several screenplays and dialogues and even contributed to song lyrics. In 1933, Parker met actor and screenwriter Alan Campbell. The two married in

61

1934, despite rumors that Campbell was bisexual – rumors that Parker herself acknowledged, claiming once that he was "queer as a billygoat" – and moved to Hollywood. Parker and Campbell worked on more than 15 films, the most noteworthy being 1937's *A Star Is Born*, which was nominated for an Academy Award for Best Writing – Screenplay. Parker also wrote additional dialogue for *The Little Foxes* in 1941, and received another Oscar nomination in 1947 for co-writing *Smash-Up, the Story of a Woman*.

In 1944, Viking Press released an anthology of Parker's works entitled *The Portable Dorothy Parker*. Initially, the book received mixed reviews, and was a mild commercial success. It remains, however, only one of three of the *Portable* series to remain continuously in print, the other two being the works of William Shakespeare and The Bible.

During the late 1930s and 1940s, Parker's political causes gradually became more of a focus in her life, as she became increasingly vocal about radical left-wing causes. She had taken an early stand against Fascism and Nazism, and helped to found the Hollywood Anti-Nazi League in 1936. In 1937, Parker reported on the Loyalist cause in Spain for the Communist publication *New Masses*, and even though she never officially joined the Communist Party, she was strongly aligned with many of its causes. This association eventually caused her to be blacklisted during the McCarthy era.

Meanwhile, Parker's marriage to Campbell continued on a rocky course. Parker continued to struggle with alcoholism and depression, and Campbell was having a long-term affair with another woman. The two divorced in 1947, then remarried in 1950. Even though they lived separately from 1952 to 1961, they remained married until Campbell's death in 1963 of "acute barbiturate poisoning," according to the coroner's report.

In her later years, Parker returned to writing book reviews, this time for *Esquire* magazine. She reviewed 208 books over the course of six years, boosting the careers of some, like Harlan Ellison, and viciously denigrating the works of others. (Parker wrote of the Beat Generation: "… if Mr. Kerouac and his followers did not think of themselves as so glorious, as intellectual as all hell and very Christlike, I should not be in such a bad humor.")

After years of moving back and forth between Hollywood and New York, Parker returned to the city she grew up in for the final time in 1963, living in the Volney residential hotel. She lived there until her death at age 73 of a heart attack.

True to her commitment to cause, Parker bequeathed her estate to the Dr. Martin Luther King, Jr. foundation. Upon King's death, her estate was passed on to the NAACP. Parker's cremated remains were buried at the NAACP headquarters in Baltimore, where a memorial garden was designed for her. The plaque reads, in part:

"Here lie the ashes of Dorothy Parker – humorist, writer, critic. Defender of human and civil rights. For her epitaph she suggested, 'Excuse my dust.'"

63

HYMN OF HATE

I Hate Books:
They tire my eyes

There is the Account of Happy Days in Far Tahiti;
The booklet of South Sea Island resorts.
After his four weeks in the South Seas,
The author's English gets pretty rusty
And he has to keep dropping into the native dialect.
He implies that his greatest hardship
Was fighting off the advances of the local girls,
But the rest of the book
Was probably founded on fact.
You can pick up a lot of handy information
On how to serve *poi,*
And where the legend of the breadfruit tree got its start,
And how to take *kava* or let it alone.
The author says it's the only life
And as good as promises
That sometime he is going to throw over his writing,
And go end his days with Laughing Sea-pig, the half-caste
        Knockout—
Why wait?

Then there is the Little Book of Whimsical Essays;
Not a headache in a libraryful.
The author comes right out and tells his favorite foods,
And how much he likes his pipe,
And what his walking-stick means to him,—
A thrill on every page.
The essays clean up all doubt
On what the author feels when riding in the subway,
Or strolling along the Palisades.
The writer seems to be going ahead on the idea

64

That it isn't such a bad old world, after all;
He drowses along
Under the influence of Pollyanesthetics.
No one is ever known to buy the book;
You find it on the guest room night-table,
Or win it at a Five Hundred Party,
Or some one gives it to you for Easter
And follows that up by asking you how you liked it,—
Say it with raspberries!

There is the novel of Primitive Emotions;
The Last Word in Unbridled Passions—
Last but not leashed.
The author writes about sex
As if he were the boy who got up the idea
The hero and heroine may be running wild in the Sahara,
Or camping informally on a desert island,
Or just knocking around the city,
But the plot is always the same—
They never quite make the grade.
The man turns out to be the son of a nobleman,
Or the woman the world's greatest heiress,
And they marry and go to live together—
That can't hold much novelty for them.
It is but a question of time till the book is made into a movie,
Which is no blow to its writer.
People laugh it off
By admitting that it may not be the highest form of art;
But then, they plead, the author must live,—
What's the big idea?

And then there is the Realistic Novel;
Five hundred pages without a snicker.
It is practically an open secret

That the book is two dollars' worth of the author's own
experiences,
And that if he had not been through them,
It would never have been written,
Which would have been all right with me.
It presents a picture of quiet family life—
Of how little Rosemary yearns to knife Grandpa,
And Father wishes Mother were cold in her grave,
And Bobby wants to marry his big brother.
The author's idea of action
Is to make one of his characters spill the cereal.
The big scene of the book
Is the heroine's decision to make over her old taffeta.
All the characters are in a bad way;
They have a lot of trouble with their suppressions.
The author is constantly explaining that they are all being
                    stifled,—
I wish to God he'd give them the air!

> *I Hate Books:*
> *They tire my eyes.*

SUCH A PRETTY LITTLE PICTURE

Mr. Wheelock was clipping the hedge. He did not dislike doing it. If it had not been for the faintly sickish odor of the privet bloom, he would definitely have enjoyed it. The new shears were so sharp and bright, there was such a gratifying sense of something done as the young green stems snapped off and the expanse of tidy, square hedge-top lengthened. There was a lot of work to be done on it. It should have been attended to a week ago, but this was the first day that Mr. Wheelock had been able to get back from the city before dinnertime.

Clipping the hedge was one of the few domestic duties that Mr. Wheelock could be trusted with. He was notoriously poor at doing anything around the house. All the suburb knew about it — it was the source of all Mrs. Wheelock's jokes. Her most popular anecdote was of how, the past winter, he had gone out and hired a man to take care of the furnace, after a seven-years' losing struggle with it. She had an admirable memory, and often as she had related the story, she never dropped a word of it. Even now, in the late summer, she could hardly tell it for laughing.

When they were first married, Mr. Wheelock had lent himself to the fun. He had even posed as being more inefficient than he really was, to make the joke better. But he had tired of his helplessness, as a topic of conversation. All the men of Mrs. Wheelock's acquaintance, her cousins, her brother-in-law, the boys she went to high school with, the neighbors' husbands, were adept at putting up a shelf, at repairing a lock, or making a shirtwaist box.

67

Mr. Wheelock had begun to feel that there was something rather effeminate about his lack of interest in such things.

He had wanted to answer his wife, lately, when she enlivened some neighbor's dinner table with tales of his inadequacy with hammer and wrench. He had wanted to cry, "All right, suppose I'm not any good at things like that. What of it?"

He had played with the idea, had tried to imagine how his voice would sound, uttering the words. But he could think of no further argument for his case than that "What of it?" And he was a little relieved, somehow, at being able to find nothing stronger. It made it reassuringly impossible to go through with the plan of answering his wife's public railleries.

Mrs. Wheelock sat, now, on the spotless porch of the neat stucco house. Beside her was a pile of her husband's shirts and drawers, the price-tags still on them. She was going over all the buttons before he wore the garments, sewing them on more firmly. Mrs. Wheelock never waited for a button to come off before sewing it on. She worked with quick, decided movements, compressing her lips each time the thread made a slight resistance to her deft jerks.

She was not a tall woman, and since the birth of her child she had gone over from a delicate plumpness to a settled stockiness. Her brown hair, though abundant, grew in an uncertain line about her forehead. It was her habit to put it up in curlers at night, but the crimps never came out in the right place. It was arranged with perfect neatness, yet it suggested that it had been done up and got over with as quickly as possible. Passionately clean, she was always redolent of the germicidal soap she used so vigorously. She was wont to tell people, somewhat redundantly, that she never employed any sort of cosmetics. She had unlimited contempt for women who sought to reduce their weight by dieting, cutting from their menus such nourishing items as cream and puddings and cereals.

Adelaide Wheelock's friends — and she had many of them — said of her that there was no nonsense about her. They and she regarded it as a compliment.

Sister, the Wheelocks' five-year-old daughter, played quietly in the gravel path that divided the tiny lawn. She had been known as Sister since her birth, and her mother still laid plans for a brother for her. Sister's baby carriage stood waiting in the cellar, her baby clothes were stacked expectantly away in bureau drawers. But raises were infrequent at the advertising agency where Mr. Wheelock was employed, and his present salary had barely caught up to the cost of their living. They could not conscientiously regard themselves as being able to afford a son. Both Mr. and Mrs. Wheelock keenly felt his guilt in keeping the bassinet empty.

Sister was not a pretty child, though her features were straight, and her eyes would one day be handsome. The left one turned slightly in toward the nose, now, when she looked in a certain direction; they would operate as soon as she was seven. Her hair was pale and limp, and her color bad. She was a delicate little girl. Not fragile in a picturesque way, but the kind of child that must be always undergoing treatment for its teeth and its throat and obscure things in its nose. She had lately had her adenoids removed, and she was still using squares of surgical gauze instead of handkerchiefs. Both she and her mother somehow felt that these gave her a sort of prestige.

She was additionally handicapped by her frocks, which her mother bought a size or so too large, with a view to Sister's growing into them — an expectation which seemed never to be realized, for her skirts were always too long, and the shoulders of her little dresses came halfway down to her thin elbows. Yet, even discounting the unfortunate way she was dressed, you could tell, in some way, that she was never going to wear any kind of clothes well.

Mr. Wheelock glanced at her now and then as he clipped. He had never felt any fierce thrills of father-love for the child. He had been disappointed in her when she was a pale, large-headed baby, smelling of stale milk and warm rubber. Sister made him feel ill at ease, vaguely irritated him. He had had no share in her training; Mrs. Wheelock was so competent a parent that she took the places of both of them. When Sister came to him to ask his permission to do something, he always told her to wait and ask her mother about it.

He regarded himself as having the usual paternal affection for his daughter. There were times, indeed, when she had tugged sharply at his heart — when he had waited in the corridor outside the operating room; when she was still under the anesthetic, and lay little and white and helpless on her high hospital bed; once when he had accidentally closed a door upon her thumb. But from the first he had nearly acknowledged to himself that he did not like Sister as a person.

Sister was not a whining child, despite her poor health. She had always been sensible and well-mannered, amenable about talking to visitors, rigorously unselfish. She never got into trouble, like other children. She did not care much for other children. She had heard herself described as being "old-fashioned," and she knew she was delicate, and she felt that

70

these attributes rather set her above them. Besides, they were rough and careless of their bodily well-being.

Sister was exquisitely cautious of her safety. Grass, she knew, was often apt to be damp in the late afternoon, so she was careful now to stay right in the middle of the gravel path, sitting on a folded newspaper and playing one of her mysterious games with three petunias that she had been allowed to pick. Mrs. Wheelock never had to speak to her twice about keeping off wet grass, or wearing her rubbers, or putting on her jacket if a breeze sprang up. Sister was an immediately obedient child, always.

II

Mrs. Wheelock looked up from her sewing and spoke to her husband. Her voice was high and clear, resolutely good-humored. From her habit of calling instructions from her upstairs window to Sister playing on the porch below, she spoke always a little louder than was necessary.

"Daddy," she said.

She had called him Daddy since some eight months before Sister was born. She and the child had the same trick of calling his name and then waiting until he signified that he was attending before they went on with what they wanted to say.

Mr. Wheelock stopped clipping, straightened himself and turned toward her.

"Daddy," she went on, thus reassured, "I saw Mr. Ince down at the post office today when Sister and I went down to get the ten o'clock mail — there wasn't much, just a card for me from Grace Williams from that place they go to up on Cape Cod,

71

and an advertisement from some department store or other about their summer fur sale (as if I cared!), and a circular for you from the bank. I opened it; I knew you wouldn't mind.

"Anyway, I just thought I'd tackle Mr. Ince first at last about getting in our cordwood. He didn't see me at first — though I'll bet he really saw me and pretended not to — but I ran right after him. 'Oh, Mr. Ince!' I said. 'Why, hello, Mrs. Wheelock,' he said, and then he asked for you, and I told him you were finely, and everything. Then I said, 'Now, Mr. Ince,' I said, 'how about getting in that cordwood of ours? ' And he said, 'Well, Mrs. Wheelock,' he said, 'I'll get it in soon's I can, but I'm short of help right now,' he said.

"Short of help! Of course I couldn't say anything, but I guess he could tell from the way I looked at him how much I believed it. I just said, 'All right, Mr. Ince, but don't you forget us. There may be a cold snap coming on,' I said, 'and we'll be wanting a fire in the living room. Don't you forget us,' I said, and he said, no, he wouldn't.

"If that wood isn't here by Monday, I think you ought to do something about it, Daddy. There's no sense in all this putting it off, and putting it off. First thing you know there'll be a cold snap coming on, and we'll be wanting a fire in the living room, and there we'll be! You'll be sure and tend to it, won't you, Daddy? I'll remind you again Monday, if I can think of it, but there are so many things!"

Mr. Wheelock nodded and turned back to his clipping — and his thoughts. They were thoughts that had occupied much of his leisure lately. After dinner, when Adelaide was sewing or arguing with the maid, he found himself letting his magazine fall face downward on his knee, while he rolled the same idea round and round in his mind. He had got so that he looked

72

forward, through the day, to losing himself in it. He had rather welcomed the hedge-clipping; you can clip and think at the same time.

It had started with a story that he had picked up somewhere. He couldn't recall whether he had heard it or had read it — that was probably it, he thought, he had run across it in the back pages of some comic paper that someone had left on the train.

It was about a man who lived in a suburb. Every morning he had gone to the city on the 8:12, sitting in the same seat in the same car, and every evening he had gone home to his wife on the 5:17, sitting in the same seat in the same car. He had done this for twenty years of his life. And then one night he didn't come home. He never went back to his office any more. He just never turned up again. The last man to see him was the conductor on the 5:17.

"He come down the platform at the Grand Central," the man reported, "just like he done every night since I been working on this road. He put one foot on the step, and then he stopped sudden, and he said 'Oh, hell,' and he took his foot off of the step and walked away. And that's the last anybody seen of him."

Curious how that story took hold of Mr. Wheelock's fancy. He had started thinking of it as a mildly humorous anecdote; he had come to accept it as fact. He did not think the man's sitting in the same seat in the same car need have been stressed so much. That seemed unimportant. He thought long about the man's wife, wondered what suburb he had lived in. He loved to play with the thing, to try to feel what the man felt before he took his foot off the car's step. He never concerned himself with speculations as to where the man had disappeared, how he had spent the rest of his life. Mr. Wheelock was

73

absorbed in that moment when he had said "Oh, hell," and walked off. "Oh, hell" seemed to Mr. Wheelock a fine thing for him to have said, a perfect summary of the situation.

He tried thinking of himself in the man's place. But no, he would have done it from the other end. That was the real way to do it.

Some summer evening like this, say, when Adelaide was sewing on buttons, up on the porch, and Sister was playing somewhere about. A pleasant, quiet evening it must be, with the shadows lying long on the street that led from their house to the station. He would put down the garden shears, or the hose, or whatever he happened to be puttering with — not throw the thing down, you know, just put it quietly aside — and walk out of the gate and down the street, and that would be the last they'd see of him. He would time it so that he'd just make the 6:03 for the city comfortably.

He did not go ahead with it from there, much. He was not especially anxious to leave the advertising agency forever. He did not particularly dislike his work. He had been an advertising solicitor since he had gone to work at all, and he worked hard at his job and aside from that, didn't think about it much one way or the other.

It seemed to Mr. Wheelock that before he had got hold of the "Oh, hell" story he had never thought about anything much, one way or the other. But he would have to disappear from the office, too, that was certain. It would spoil everything to turn up there again. He thought dimly of taking a train going West, after the 6:03 got him to the Grand Central Terminal — he might go to Buffalo, say, or perhaps Chicago. Better just let that part take care of itself and go back to dwell on the moment when it would sweep over him that he was going to do it, when he would put down the shears and walk out the gate —

The "Oh, hell" rather troubled him. Mr. Wheelock felt that he would like to retain that; it completed the gesture so beautifully. But he didn't quite know to whom he should say it.

He might stop in at the post office on his way to the station and say it to the postmaster; but the postmaster would probably think he was only annoyed at there being no mail for him. Nor would the conductor of the 6:03, a train Mr. Wheelock never used, take the right interest in it. Of course the real thing to do would be to say it to Adelaide just before he laid down the shears. But somehow Mr. Wheelock could not make that scene come very clear in his imagination.

III

"Daddy," Mrs. Wheelock said briskly.

He stopped clipping, and faced her.

"Daddy," she related, "I saw Doctor Mann's automobile going by the house this morning — he was going to have a look at Mr. Warren, his rheumatism's getting along nicely — and I called him in a minute, to look us over."

She screwed up her face, winked, and nodded vehemently several times in the direction of the absorbed Sister, to indicate that she was the subject of the discourse.

"He said we were going ahead finely," she resumed, when she was sure that he had caught the idea. "Said there was no need for those t-o-n-s-i-l-s to c-o-m-e o-u-t. But I thought, soon's it gets a little cooler, some time next month, we'd just

75

run in to the city and let Doctor Sturges have a look at us. I'd rather be on the safe side."

"But Doctor Lytton said it wasn't necessary, and those doctors at the hospital, and now Doctor Mann, that's known her since she was a baby," suggested Mr. Wheelock.

"I know, I know," replied his wife. "But I'd rather be on the safe side."

Mr. Wheelock went back to his hedge.

Oh, of course he couldn't do it; he never seriously thought he could, for a minute. Of course he couldn't. He wouldn't have the shadow of an excuse for doing it. Adelaide was a sterling woman, an utterly faithful wife, an almost slavish mother. She ran his house economically and efficiently. She harried the suburban trades people into giving them dependable service, drilled the succession of poorly paid, poorly trained maids, cheerfully did the thousand fussy little things that go with the running of a house. She looked after his clothes, gave him medicine when she thought he needed it, oversaw the preparation of every meal that was set before him; they were not especially inspirational meals, but the food was always nourishing and, as a general thing, fairly well cooked. She never lost her temper, she was never depressed, never ill.

Not the shadow of an excuse. People would know that, and so they would invent an excuse for him. They would say there must be another woman.

Mr. Wheelock frowned, and snipped at an obstinate young twig. Good Lord, the last thing he wanted was another woman. What he wanted was that moment when he realized he could do it, when he would lay down the shears —

76

Oh, of course he couldn't; he knew that as well as anybody. What would they do, Adelaide and Sister? The house wasn't even paid for yet, and there would be that operation on Sister's eye in a couple of years. But the house would be all paid up by next March. And there was always that well-to-do brother-in-law of Adelaide's, the one who, for all his means, put up every shelf in that great big house with his own hands.

Decent people didn't just go away and leave their wives and families that way. All right, suppose you weren't decent; what of it? Here was Adelaide planning what she was going to do when it got a little cooler, next month. She was always planning ahead, always confident that things would go on just the same. Naturally, Mr. Wheelock realized that he couldn't do it, as well as the next one. But there was no harm in fooling around with the idea. Would you say the "Oh, hell" now, before you laid down the shears, or right after? How would it be to turn at the gate and say it?

Mr. and Mrs. Fred Coles came down the street arm-in-arm, from their neat stucco house on the corner.

"See they've got you working hard, eh?" cried Mr. Coles genially, as they paused abreast of the hedge.

Mr. Wheelock laughed politely, marking time for an answer.

"That's right," he evolved.

Mrs. Wheelock looked up from her work, shading her eyes with her thimbled hand against the long rays of the low sun.

77

"Yes, we finally got Daddy to do a little work," she called brightly. "But Sister and I are staying right here to watch over him, for fear he might cut his little self with the shears."

There was general laughter, in which Sister joined. She had risen punctiliously at the approach of the older people, and she was looking politely at their eyes, as she had been taught.

"And how is my great big girl?" asked Mrs. Coles, gazing fondly at the child.

"Oh, much better," Mrs. Wheelock answered for her. "Doctor Mann says we are going ahead finely. I saw his automobile passing the house this morning — he was going to see Mr. Warren, his rheumatism's coming along nicely — and I called him in a minute to look us over."

She did the wink and the nods, at Sister's back. Mr. and Mrs. Coles nodded shrewdly back at her.

"He said there's no need for those t-o-n-s-i-l-s to c-o-m-e o-u-t," Mrs. Wheelock called. "But I thought, soon's it gets a little cooler, some time next month, we'd just run in to the city and let Doctor Sturges have a look at us. I was telling Daddy, 'I'd rather be on the safe side,' I said."

"Yes, it's better to be on the safe side," agreed Mrs. Coles, and her husband nodded again, sagely this time. She took his arm, and they moved slowly off.

"Been a lovely day, hasn't it?" she said over her shoulder, fearful of having left too abruptly. "Fred and I are taking a little constitutional before supper."

"Oh, taking a little constitutional?" cried Mrs. Wheelock, laughing.

Mrs. Coles laughed also, three or four bars.

"Yes, just taking a little constitutional before supper," she called back.

Sister, weary of her game, mounted the porch, whimpering a little. Mrs. Wheelock put aside her sewing, and took the tired child in her lap. The sun's last rays touched her brown hair, making it a shimmering gold. Her small, sharp face, the thick lines of her figure were in shadow as she bent over the little girl. Sister's head was hidden on her mother's shoulder, the folds of her rumpled white frock followed her limp, relaxed little body.

The lovely light was kind to the cheap, hurriedly built stucco house, to the clean gravel path, and the bits of closely cut lawn. It was gracious, too, to Mr. Wheelock's tall, lean figure as he bent to work on the last few inches of unclipped hedge.

Twenty years, he thought. The man in the story went through with it for twenty years. He must have been a man along around forty-five, most likely. Mr. Wheelock was thirty-seven. Eight years. It's a long time, eight years is. You could easily get so you could say that final "Oh, hell," even to Adelaide, in eight years. It probably wouldn't take more than four for you to know that you could do it. No, not more than two...

Mrs. Coles paused at the corner of the street and looked back at the Wheelocks' house. The last of the light lingered on the mother and child group on the porch, gently touched the tall, white-clad figure of the husband and father as he went up to them, his work done.

Mrs. Coles was a large, soft woman, barren, and addicted to sentiment.

"Look, Fred; just turn around and look at that," she said to her husband. She looked again, sighing luxuriously. "Such a pretty little picture!"

When a woman hears a man railing at matrimony, she agrees with him first and marries him later.

MEN I'M NOT MARRIED TO

No matter where my route may lie,
   No matter whither I repair,
In brief — no matter how or why
   Or when I go, the boys are there.
On lane and byways, street and square,
   On alley, path and avenue,
They seem to spring up everywhere —
   The men I am not married to.

I watch them as they pass me by;
   At each in wonderment I stare,
And, "but for heaven's grace," I cry,
   "There goes the guy whose name I'd
     wear!"
They represent no species rare,
   They walk and talk as others do;
They're fair to see but only fair
   The men I am not married to.

I'm sure that to a mother's eye
   Is each potentially a bear.
But though at home they rank ace-high,
   No change of heart could I declare.
Yet worry silvers not their hair;
   They deck them not with sprigs of rue.
It's curious how they do not care
   The men I am not married to.

L'ENVOI

In fact, if they'd a chance to share
   Their lot with me, a lifetime through,
They'd doubtless tender me the air
   The men I am not married to.

81

FREDDIE

"Oh, boy!" people say of Freddie. "You just ought to meet him some time! He's a riot, that's what he is – more fun than a goat."

Other, and more imaginative souls play whimsically with the idea, and say that he is more fun than a barrel of monkeys. Still others go at the thing from a different angle, and refer to him as being as funny as a crutch. But I always feel, myself, that they stole the line from Freddie. Satire – that is his dish.

And there you have, really, one of Freddie's greatest crosses. People steal his stuff right and left. He will say something one day, and the next it will be as good as all over the city. Time after time I have gone to him and told him that I have heard lots of vaudeville acts using his comedy, but he just puts on the most killing expression, and says, "Oh, say not suchly!" in that way of his. And, of course, it gets me laughing so that I can't say another word about it.

That is the way he always is, just laughing it off when he is told that people are using his best lines without even so much as word of acknowledgment. I never hear anyone say, "There is such a thing as being too good-natured," but that I think of Freddie.

You never knew any one like him at a party. Things will be dragging along, the way they do at the beginning of the evening, with the early arrivals sitting around asking one another have they been to anything good at the theatre lately, and is it any wonder there is so much sickness around with the weather so changeable. The party will be just about plucking at the coverlet when in will breeze Freddie, and from that moment on the evening is little short of a whirlwind. Often and often I have heard him called the life of the party, and I have always felt that there is not the least bit of exaggeration in the expression.

What I envy about Freddie is that poise of his. He can come right into a room full of strangers, and be just as much at home as if he had gone through grammar school with them. He smashes the ice all to nothing the moment he is introduced to the other guests by pretending to misunderstand their names, and calling them something entirely different, keeping a perfectly straight face all the time as if he never realized there was anything wrong. A great many people say he puts them in mind of Buster Keaton that way.

He is never at a loss for a screaming crack. If the hostess asks him to have a chair Freddie comes right back at her with "No, thanks; we have chairs at home." If the host offers him a cigar he will say just like a flash, "What's the matter with it?" If one of the men borrows a cigarette and a light from him Freddie will say in that dry voice of his, "Do you want the coupons too?" Of course his wit is pretty fairly caustic, but no one ever seems to take offense at it. I suppose there is everything in the way he says things.

And he is practically a whole vaudeville show in himself. He is never without a new story of what Pat said to Mike as they were walking down the street, or how Abie tried to cheat Ikie, or what old Aunt Jemima answered when she was asked why she had married for the fifth time. Freddie does them in dialect, and I have often thought it is a wonder that we don't all split our sides. And never a selection that every member of the family couldn't listen to, either – just healthy fun.

Then he has a repertory of song numbers, too. He gives them without accompaniment, and every song has a virtually unlimited number of verses, after each one of which Freddie goes conscientiously through the chorus. There is one awfully clever one, a big favorite of his, with the chorus rendered a different way each time showing how they sang it when grandma was a girl, how they sing it in gay Paree and how a cabaret performer would do it.

Then there are several along the general lines of Casey Jones, two or three about negroes who specialized on the banjo, and a few in which the lyric of the chorus consists of the syllables "ha, ha, ha." The idea is that the audience will get laughing along with the singer.

If there is a piano in the house Freddie can tear things even wider open. There may be many more accomplished musicians, but nobody can touch him as far as being ready to oblige goes. There is never any of this hanging back waiting to be coaxed or protesting that he hasn't touched a key in months. He just sits right down and does all his specialties for you. He is particularly good at doing "Dixie" with one hand and "Home, Sweet Home" with the other, and Josef Hofmann himself can't tie Freddie when it comes to giving an imitation of a fife-and-drum corps approaching, passing, and fading away in the distance.

But it is when the refreshments are served that Freddie reaches the top of his form. He always insists on helping to pass plates and glasses, and when he gets a big armful of them he pretends to stumble. It is as good as a play to see the hostess' face. Then he tucks his napkin into his collar, and sits there just as solemnly as if he thought that were the thing to do; or perhaps he will vary that one by folding the napkin into a little square and putting it carefully in his pocket,

84

as if he thought it was a handkerchief. You just ought to see him making believe that he has swallowed an olive pit. And the remarks he makes about the food I do wish I could remember how they go. He is funniest, though, it seems to me, when he is pretending that the lemonade is intoxicating, and that he feels its effects pretty strongly. When you have seen him do this it will be small surprise to you that Freddie is in such demand for social functions.

But Freddie is not one of those humourists who perform only when out in society. All day long he is bubbling over with fun. And the beauty of it is that he is not a mere theorist, as a joker; practical – that's Freddie all over.

If he isn't sending long telegrams, collect, to his friends, then he is sending them packages of useless groceries, C. O. D. A telephone is just so much meat to him. I don't believe any one will ever know how much fun Freddie and his friends get out of Freddie's calling them up and making them guess who he is. When he really wants to extend himself he calls up in the middle of the night, and says that he is the wire tester. He uses that one only on special occasions, though. It is pretty elaborate for everyday use.

But day in and day out, you can depend upon it that he is putting over some uproarious trick with a dribble glass or a loaded cigar or a pencil with a rubber point; and you can feel completely sure that no matter where he is or how unexpectedly you may come upon him, Freddie will be right there with a funny line or a comparatively new story for you. That is what people marvel over when they are talking about him how he is always just the same.

It is right there, really, that they put their finger on the big trouble with him.

But you just ought to meet Freddie sometime. He's a riot, that's what he is – more fun than a circus.

MORTIMER

Mortimer had his photograph taken in his dress suit.

RAYMOND

So long as you keep him well inland Raymond will never give any trouble. But when he gets down to the seashore he affects a bathing suit fitted with little sleeves. On wading into the sea ankle-deep he leans over and carefully applies handfuls of water to his wrists and forehead.

CHARLIE

It's curious, but no one seems to be able to recall what Charlie used to talk about before the country went what may be called, with screaming effect, dry. Of course there must have been a lot of unsatisfactory weather even then, and I don't doubt that he slipped in a word or two when the talk got around to the insanity of the then-current styles of women's dress.
But though I have taken up the thing in a serious way, and have gone about among his friends making inquiries, I cannot seem to find that he could ever have got any farther than that in the line of conversation. In fact, he must have been one of those strong silent men in the old days.

Those who have not seen him for several years would be in a position to be knocked flat with a feather if they could see what a regular little chatterbox Charlie has become. Say what you will about prohibition –and who has a better right? –

you would have to admit, if you knew Charlie, that it has been the making of him as a conversationalist.

He never requires his audience to do any feeding for him. It needs no careful leading around of the subject, no tactful questions, no well-timed allusions, to get him nicely loosened up. All you have to do is say good evening to him, ask him how everybody over at his house is getting along, and give him a chair – though this last is not essential – and silver-tongued Charlie is good for three hours straight on where he is getting it, how much he has to pay for it, and what the chances are of his getting hold of a couple of cases of genuine pinch-bottle, along around the middle of next week. I have known him to hold entire dinner parties spellbound, from cocktails to finger bowls, with his monologue.

Now I would be well down among the last when it came to wanting to give you the impression that Charlie has been picked for the All-American alcoholic team. Despite the wetness of his conversation he is just a nice, normal, conscientious drinker, willing to take it or let it alone, in the order named. I don't say he would not be able to get along without it, but neither do I say that he doesn't get along perfectly splendidly with it. I don't think I ever saw any one who could get as much fun as Charlie can out of splitting the Eighteenth Amendment with a friend.

There is a glamour of vicarious romance about him. You gather from his conversation that he comes into daily contact with any number of picturesque people. He tells about a friend of his who owns three untouched bottles of the last absinth to come into the country; or a lawyer he knows, one of whose grateful clients sent him six cases of champagne in addition to his fee; or a man he met who had to move to the country in order to have room for his Scotch.

87

Charlie has no end of anecdotes about the interesting women he meets, too. There is one girl he often dwells on, who, if you only give her time, can get you little bottles of chartreuse, each containing an individual drink. Another gifted young woman friend of his is the inventor of a cocktail in which you mix a spoonful of orange marmalade. Yet another is the justly proud owner of a pet marmoset which becomes the prince of good fellows as soon as you have fed him a couple of teaspoonfuls of gin.

It is the next best thing to knowing these people yourself to hear Charlie tell about them. He just makes them live.

It is wonderful how Charlie's circle of acquaintances has widened during the last two years; there is nothing so broadening as prohibition. Among his new friends he numbers a conductor on a train that runs down from Montreal, and a young man who owns his own truck, and a group of chaps who work in drug stores, and I don't know how many proprietors of homey little restaurants in the basements of brownstone houses.

Some of them have turned out to be but fair-weather friends, unfortunately. There was one young man, whom Charlie had looked upon practically as a brother, who went particularly bad on him. It seems he had taken a pretty solemn oath to supply Charlie, as a personal favour, with a case of real Gordon, which he said he was able to get through his high social connections on the other side. When what the young man called a nominal sum was paid, and the case was delivered, its bottles were found to contain a nameless liquor, though those of Charlie's friends who gave it a fair trial suggested Storm King as a good name for the brand. Charlie has never laid eyes on the young man from that day to this. He is still unable to talk about it without a break in his voice. As he says – and quite rightly, too – it was the principle of the thing.

But for the most part his new friends are just the truest pals a man ever had. In more time than it takes to tell it, Charlie will keep you right abreast with them sketch in for you how they are, and what they are doing, and what their last words to him were.

But Charlie can be the best of listeners, too. Just tell him about any little formula you may have picked up for making it at home, and you will find the most sympathetic of audiences, and one who will even go to the flattering length of taking notes on your discourse. Relate to him tales of unusual places where you have heard that you can get it or of grotesque sums that you have been told have been exchanged for it, and he will hang on your every word, leading you on, asking intelligent questions, encouraging you by references to like experiences of his own.

But don't let yourself get carried away with success and attempt to branch out into other topics. For you will lose Charlie in a minute if you try it.

But that, now I think of it, would probably be the very idea you would have in mind.

LLOYD

Lloyd wears washable neckties.

HENRY

You would really be surprised at the number of things that Henry knows just a shade more about than anybody else does. Naturally he can't help realizing this about himself, but you mustn't think for a minute that he has let it spoil him. On the contrary, as the French so well put it. He has no end of patience with others, and he is always willing to oversee what they are doing, and to offer them counsel. When it comes to giving his time and his energy there is nobody who could not admit that Henry is generous. To a fault, I have even heard people go so far as to say.

If, for instance, Henry happens to drop in while four of his friends are struggling along through a game of bridge he does not cut in and take a hand, thereby showing up their playing in comparison to his. No, Henry draws up a chair and sits looking on with a kindly smile. Of course, now and then he cannot restrain a look of pain or an exclamation of surprise or even a burst of laughter as he listens to the bidding, but he never interferes. Frequently, after a card has been played, he will lean over and in a good-humoured way tell the player what he should have done instead, and how he might just as well throw his hand down then and there, but he always refuses to take any more active part in the game. Occasionally, when a uniquely poisonous play is made, I have seen Henry thrust his chair aside and pace about in speechless excitement, but for the most part he is admirably self-controlled. He always leaves with a few cheery words to the players, urging them to keep at it and not let themselves get discouraged.

And that is the way Henry is about everything. He will stroll over to a tennis court, and stand on the side lines, at what I am sure must be great personal inconvenience, calling words of advice and suggestion for sets at a stretch. I have even known him to follow his friends all the way around a golf course, offering constructive criticism on their form as he goes. I tell you, in this day and generation, you don't find many people who will go as far out of their way for their friends as Henry does. And I am far from being the only one who says so, too.

I have often thought that Henry must be the boy who got up the idea of leaving the world a little better than he found it. Yet he never crashes in on his friends' affairs. Only after the thing is done does he point out to you how it could have been done just a dash better. After you have signed the lease for the new apartment Henry tells you where you could have got one cheaper and sunnier; after you are all tied up with the new firm Henry explains to you where you made your big mistake in leaving the old one.

It is never any news to me when I hear people telling Henry that he knows more about more things than anybody they ever saw in their lives.

And I don't remember ever having heard Henry give them any argument on that one.

JOE

After Joe had had two cocktails he wanted to go up and bat for the trap drummer. After he had had three he began to get personal about the unattractive shade of the necktie worn by the strange man at the next table.

OLIVER

Oliver had a way of dragging his mouth to one side, by means of an inserted forefinger, explaining to you,

91

meanwhile, in necessarily obscured tones, the work which his dentist had just accomplished on his generously displayed back teeth.

ALBERT

Albert sprinkled powdered sugar on his sliced tomatoes.

Franklin Pierce Adams

1881–1960

*"Having imagination it takes you an hour to write a paragraph
that if you were unimaginative would take you only a minute."*

Franklin Leopold Adams was born on November 15,
1881, in Chicago, Illinois to dry goods merchant Moses Adams
and his wife Clara. It wasn't until his confirmation at age 13
did young Frank change his middle name to Pierce, after 14th
President of the United States Franklin Pierce. Adams attended
the Armour Scientific Academy in Chicago, where he
graduated in 1899.

Adams went to college at the University of Michigan at
Ann Arbor, but only for a year, when financial difficulties
forced him to leave school. He returned to Chicago, selling
insurance to supplement his family's income. Adams' turn as
an insurance agent was fortuitous, as one of his first customers
was George Ade, a local newspaper columnist, playwright, and
humorist. Inspired by Ade, Adams decided to try his hand at
journalism, and his first printed work appeared in the *Chicago
Journal* as verses in the paper's "Poet's Corner." A small
volume of his poems, entitled *In Cupid's Court* was published
in 1902. With these small successes under his belt, Adams quit
the insurance industry and began work at the *Chicago Tribune*
as a columnist in 1903.

The following year, Adams moved to New York and began writing a column for the *New York Evening Mail*. His tenure there lasted for nine years, during which he wrote what is arguably his best known work, *Baseball's Sad Lexicon*, a tribute to the Chicago Cubs double play combination of "Tinker to Evers to Chance." From there, he moved to the *New York Tribune* and began writing a column he called "The Conning Tower," a reference to the raised structure on a submarine used for navigation. The name stuck for the rest of his career. Adams also began signing the end of his columns with his initials, thus he was always referred to as "FPA" from that point forward.

For a brief period of time during World War I, FPA was enlisted in the United States Army, writing for the *Stars and Stripes*. Here he worked alongside future co-Round Tablers Harold Ross and Alexander Woollcott. After his military stint was over, FPA returned to the *Tribune*, and he soon gained a reputation for helping launch the careers of several promising new writers. He invited his readers to submit contributions, many of which he would publish in "The Conning Tower." Among those promoted by FPA were such future literary giants as Robert Benchley, James Thurber, Eugene O'Neill, E.B. White, and Dorothy Parker. In giving credit to FPA, Parker once said that he had "raised her from a couplet."

Apart from his dedication to his long-running column, which ran in various New York newspapers until it ended its run in September 1941, FPA had fairly modest literary ambitions; almost all of his published books were compiled from prose and poetry previously printed in "The Conning Tower." In 1938, FPA began to make appearances on the popular radio program "Information, Please!" in which a panel of experts answered questions sent in by listeners. If the panelists could not answer a question correctly, the listener was

94

rewarded a set of encyclopedias. FPA was the designated expert on poetry, old bar-room songs, and Gilbert and Sullivan. He remained a regular on the show until 1948.

During his life, FPA was married twice, with both marriages ending in divorce. His second marriage produced four children, and though he wrote tender poems about them, he was reported to be a distant and aloof father. One of his children was even heard to remark that anyone who had read "The Conning Tower" knew as much about FPA as they did.

Starting in the late 1940's, FPA was given to bouts of memory loss and temper outbursts, most likely due to the onset and progression of Alzheimer's disease. Over the years, he was increasingly unable to take care of himself, and was eventually placed in a New York City nursing home, where he died on March 23, 1960.

WOMEN I'M NOT MARRIED TO

"Whene'er I take my walks" — you know
 The rest — "abroad," I always meet
Elaine or Maude or Anne or Flo,
 Belinda, Blanche, or Marguerite;
And Melancholy, bittersweet,
 Sets seal upon me when I view —
Coldly, and from a judgment seat —
 The women I'm not married to.

Not mine the sighs for Long Ago;
 Not mine to mourn the obsolete;
With Burns and Shelley, Keats and Poe
 I have no yearning to compete.
No Dead Sea pickled pears I eat;
 I never touch a drop of rue;
I toast, and drink my pleasure neat,
 The women I'm not married to!

Fate with her celebrated blow
 Frequently knocks me off my feet;
And Life her dice box chucks a throw
 That usually has me beat.
Yet although Love has tried to treat
 Me rough, award the kid his due.
Look at the list, though incomplete:
 The women I'm not married to.

L'ENVOI

My dears whom gracefully I greet,
 Gaze at these lucky ladies who
Are of — to make this thing concrete —
 The women I'm not married to.

ELAINE

There have been more beautiful girls than Elaine, for I have read about them, and I have utter faith in the printed word. And I expect my public, a few of whom are – just a second – more than two and a quarter million weekly, to put the same credence in my printed word. When I said there have been more beautiful girls than Elaine I lied. There haven't been. She was a darb. Blue were her eyes as the fairy flax, her eyebrows were like curved snowdrifts, her neck was like the swan, her face it was the fairest that e'er the sun shone on, she walked in beauty like the night, her lips were like the cherries ripe that sunny walls of Boreas screen, her teeth were like a flock of sheep with fleeces newly washen clean, her hair was like the curling mist that shades the mountain side at e'en, and oh, she danced in such a way no sun upon an Easter day was half so fine a sight! If I may interrupt the poets, I should say she was one pip. She was, I might add, kind of pretty.

Enchantment was hers, and fairyland her exclusive province. I would walk down a commonplace street with her, and it would become the primrose path, and a one-way path at that, with nobody but us on it. If I said it was a nice day – and if I told her that once I told her a hundred times – she would say, "Isn't it? My very words to Isabel when I telephoned her this morning!" So we had, I said to myself, a lot in common.

And after a conversation like that I would go home and lie awake and think, "If two persons can be in such harmony about the weather, a fundamental thing, a thing that prehistoric religions actually were based upon, what possible discord ever could be between us? For I have known families to be rent by disagreements as to meteorological conditions.

"Isn't this," my sister used to say, "a nice day?"

97

"No," my reply used to be; "it's a dreadful day. It's blowy, and it's going to rain." And I would warn my mother that my sister Amy, or that child, was likely to grow up into a liar.

But, as I have tried to hint, beauty was Elaine's, and when she spoke of the weather I used to feel sorry for everybody who had lived in the olden times, from yesterday back to the afternoon Adam told Eve that no matter how hot it was they always got a breeze, before there was any weather at all.

It wasn't only the weather. We used to agree on other things. Once when she met a schoolgirl friend in Hyde Park whom she hadn't seen since a year ago, out in Lake View, she said that it was a small world after all, and I told her she never said a truer word. And about golf – she didn't think, she said one day, that it was as strenuous as tennis, but it certainly took you out in the open air – well, that was how I felt about it, too. So you see it wasn't just the weather, though at that time I thought that would be enough.

Well, one day we were walking along, and she looked at me and said, "I wonder if you'd like me so much if I weren't pretty."

It came over me that I shouldn't.

"No," I said, "I should say not."

"That's the first honest thing you ever said to me," she said.

"No, it isn't," I said.

"It is, too," was her rejoinder.

"It's nothing of the kind," I said.

"Yes, it is!" she said, her petulant temper getting the better of her.

So we parted on that, and I often think how lucky I am to have escaped from Elaine's distrust of honesty, and from her violent and passionate temper.

MAUDE

Maude and I might have been happy together. She was not the kind you couldn't be candid with. She used to say she admired honesty and sincerity above all other traits. And she was deeply interested in me, which was natural enough, as I had no reservations, no reticences from her. I believed that when you cared about a girl it was wrong to have secrets from her.

And that was her policy, too, though now and then she carried it too far. One day I telephoned her and asked her what she had been doing that morning.

"I've been reading the most fascinating book," she said.

"What book?" I asked politely.

"I can't remember the title," she said, "but it's about a man in love with a girl, and he . . ."

"Who wrote it?" I interrupted.

"Wait a minute," said Maude. I waited four minutes. "Sorry to have kept you waiting," she said. "I mislaid the book. I thought I left it in my room and I looked all around for it, and then I asked Hulda if she'd seen it, and she said no, though I asked her that the other day about something else, and she said no, and later I found out that she had seen it and put it in a drawer, so I went to the library and the book wasn't there, and then I went back to my room and looked again, and I was just coming back to tell you I couldn't find it when here it is, guess where, right on the telephone stand. Who wrote it? Hutchison is the author. A. M. S. – no, wait a minute – A. S. M. Hutchinson, not Hutchison. There's an 'n' in it. Two 'n's' really. But I mean an 'n' between the 'i' and the 's.' I mean it's Hut-chin-son, and not Hut-chi-son. But what's the difference who writes a book as long as it's a good book?"

There may have been more, but I was reasonably certain that the author's name was Hutchinson, so I hung up the receiver, though the way I felt at the time was that hanging was too good for it.

I had dinner with her that night at a restaurant.

"Coffee?" asked the waiter.

"No," I said. And to her: "Coffee keeps me awake. If I took a cup now I wouldn't close an eye all night. Some folks can drink it and not notice it, but take me; I'm funny that way, and if I took a cup now I wouldn't close an eye all night. Some can, and some can't. I like it, but it doesn't like me. Ha, ha! I wouldn't close an eye all night, and if I don't get my sleep – and a good eight hours at that – I'm not fit for a thing all the next day. It's a pretty important thing, sleep; and… "

It was important to Maude, self-centered thing that she was. Here was I confiding to her something I never had told another soul, and she wasn't merely dozing; she was asleep. I rattled a knife against a plate, and she awoke.

It was a good thing I found out about her in time.

ANNE

In winter, when the ground was white,
I thought that Anne would be all right;
In summer, quite the other way,
I knew she'd never be O. K.

She liked to go to the theatre, but what she went for was to be amused, as there was enough sadness in real life without going to the theatre for it. She told me that I was just a great big boy; that all men, in fact, were just little boys grown up. I took her to a movie show, and she read most of the captions to me, slowly; and when she read them to herself her lips moved. She never took a drink in days of old when booze was sold and barrooms held their sway – that is my line, not Anne's – but now she takes a cocktail when one is offered, saying, "This may be my last chance." Women, she told me, didn't like her much, but she didn't care, as she was, she always said, a man's woman. Just the same, folks said, she told me, that she was wonderful in a sick room. And so, what with the movies and one thing and another the winter passed. She was glad I was a tennis player, and we'd have some exciting sets in the summer. No, she said games. I should have known then, but I was thinking of her hair and how cool it was to stroke.

Well, one May afternoon there we were on the tennis court. It belonged to a friend of hers, and it hadn't been rolled

101

recently, nor marked, though you could tell that here a base line and there a service line once had been.

I asked her which court she wanted and she said it didn't matter; she played equally rottenly on both sides. Nor was that, I found it, overstating things. She served, and called "Ready?" before each service. When she sent a ball far outside she called "Home run!" or "Just out!" And if I served a double fault she said either "Two bad" or "Thank you." When the score was deuce she called it "Juice!" And when I beat her 6-0 − as you could have done, or you, or even you − she said she was off her game, that it was a lot closer than the score indicated, that she'd beat me before the summer was over, that didn't the net seem terribly low or something, and that I wasn't used to playing with women or I wouldn't hit the ball so hard all the time.

Little remains to be told. Anne is now the wife of a golfing banker. Wednesday night I met her at a party.

"Golf?" she echoed. "Oh, yes. That is, I don't play it; I play at it. Tennis is really my game, but I haven't had a racket in my hand in two years. We must have some of our games again. I nearly beat you last time, remember."

FLO

I hadn't seen Flo since she was about fourteen, so when I got a letter asking me to call I said I'd go. She was pretty, but the older I get the fewer girls I see that aren't.

Of course I ought to have known. The letter was addressed with a "For" preceding my name, instead of "City" or the name of the town, Flo had written "Local." Even a professional detective should have known then.

It was just her refined vocabulary that sent me reeling into the night. She wondered where I "resided" and how long I'd been "located" there; she had "purchased" something; she said "gowned" when she meant "dressed"; she had "gotten" tired, she said, of affectation. She said she had "retired" early the night before, and she spoke of a "boot-limber."

And as I was leaving she said, "Don't remain away so long this time. Er – you know – hath no fury like a woman scorned."

BELINDA

I remember Belinda. She was arguing with another young woman about the car fare. "Let me pay," said Belinda; and she paid.

"There," I mused, "is a perfect woman, nobly planned."

I met her shortly after that, and she came through many a test. Once I saw her go up to an elevated railroad station, hand in a nickel, and not say, "One, please." Once I asked her about what day it was, and she said "Wednesday" without adding "All day." She spoke once of a cultivated taste without adding "like olives," and once said "That's another story" without adding "as Kipling says." And once – and that was the day I nearly begged her to be mine – when she said that something had been grossly exaggerated she failed to giggle "like the report of Mark Twain's death."

So you see Belinda had points. She had a dog that wasn't more intelligent than most human beings; she wasn't forever saying that there was no reason why a man and a

103

woman shouldn't be just good pals; she didn't put me at ease, the way the others did, by looking at me for three minutes and then saying that good looks didn't matter much to a man, after all; she didn't, when you gave her something, take it and say coyly, "For me?" as who should say, "You dear thoughtful thing, when you might have brought it for John D. Rockefeller." And she didn't say that she couldn't draw a straight line or that she had no card sense or that she couldn't write a decent letter.

She could write a decent letter. She did. Lots of them. To me, too. She wrote the best letters I ever read. They were intelligent, humorous, and – why shouldn't I tell the truth? – ardent. Fervid is nearer. Candescent is not far off. And that is how I lost her.

"P. S." she wrote. "Burn this letter, and all of them."

A few weeks later Belinda said, "At the rate I write you, my letters must fill a large drawer by this time."

"Why," I said, "I burn them. They're all burned."

"I never want to see you again as long as I live," she said. "Good-by."

And my good-by was the last communication between me and Belinda.

BLANCHE

Blanche is a girl
  I'd hate to wed,
Because of a lot
  Of things she said.

104

"Excuse my French"
  When she says "Gee-whiz!"
On the telephone:
  "Guess who this is."

You ask her did
  She like the show
Or book, she'll say,
  "Well, yes and no.'

For the "kiddie" she
  Buys a "comfy" "nighty";
She says "My bestest,"
  And "All rightie"

"If I had no humour,
  I'd simply die,"
Says Blanche. ... I know
  That that's a lie.

She wouldn't marry;
  "Oh, heaven forbid!
"Men are such brutes!"
  You said it, kid.

MARGUERITE

Marguerite was an agreer. She strove, and not without success, to please. She hated an argument, one reason perhaps being – I found this out later – that she couldn't put one forth on any subject. But I had theories, in the days of Marguerite, and I wanted to know whether she was in sympathy with them. One of my theories was that a lot of domestic infelicity could be avoided if a husband didn't keep his business affairs to

105

himself, if he made a confidante, a possible assistant, of his wife. I had contempt for the women whose boast it was that Fred never brings business into the house.

So I used to talk to Marguerite about that theory. When we were married wouldn't it be better to discuss the affairs of the business day at home with her? Certainly. Because simply talking about them was something, and maybe she could even help. Yes, that was what a wife was for. Why should a man keep his thoughts bottled up just because his wife wasn't in his office with him? No reason at all; I agree with you perfectly.

About politics: Wasn't this man Harding doing a good job, and weren't things looking pretty good, everything considered? He certainly is and they certainly are, was Marguerite's adroit summing up.

Well, I had theories about books and child labor and pictures and clam chowder and Harry Leon Wilson's stuff and music and the younger generation and cord tires and things like that, and she'd agree with everything I said.

Then one night, as in a vision, something came to me. I had a theory that it would be terrible to have somebody around all the time who agreed with you about everything. Marguerite agreed.

I had another theory. Don't you agree, I put it, that we shouldn't get along at all well? And never had she agreed more quickly. I thought she really put her heart into it.

And we never should have hit it off, either.

US POETS

Wordsworth wrote some tawdry stuff;
  Much of Moore I have forgotten;
Parts of Tennyson are guff;
  Bits of Byron, too, are rotten.

All of Browning isn't great;
  There are slipshod lines in Shelley;
Every one knows Homer's fate;
  Some of Keats is vermicelli.

Sometimes Shakespeare hit the slide,
  Not to mention Pope or Milton;
Some of Southey's stuff is snide.
  Some of Spenser's simply Stilton.

When one has to boil the pot,
  One can't always watch the kittle.
You may credit it or not –
  Now and then *I* slump a little!

OUR DUMB'D ANIMALS

What time I seek my virtuous couch to steal
  Some surcease from the labours of the day,
Ere silence like a poultice comes to heal –
  In short, when I prepare to hit the hay;
Ere slumber's chains (I quote from Moore) have bound me,
  I hear a lot of noises all around me.

Time was when falling off the well-known log
  Were harder far than falling off to sleep;
But that was ere my neighbour's gentle dog
  Began to think he was defending sheep.
From twelve to two his barking and his howling
Accompanies two torn cats' nightly yowling.

At two-ten sharp the parrot in the flat
  Across the way his monologue essays.
At three, again, as Gilbert says, the cat;
  At four a milkman's horse, exulted, neighs.
At six-fifteen, nor does it ever vary,
  I hear the dulcet tones of a canary.

Each living thing I love; I love the birds;
  The beasts in field and forest, too, I love,
But I have writ these poor, if metric words,
  To query which, by all the pow'rs above,
Of all the animals – pray tell me, some one –
  Is called by any courtesy a dumb one?

Heywood Broun

1888–1939

"The great threat to the young and pure in heart is not what they read but what they don't read."

Heywood Campbell Broun was born on December 7 in Brooklyn, New York to Henriette and Heywood Cox Broun, an English immigrant who developed and ran a successful printing business in the city. Heywood Broun graduated high school at the Horace Mann School in Riverdale, New York, and then continued his higher education at Harvard University beginning in 1907. Because he did not fare well in foreign languages – most noticeably French, which he failed repeatedly – Broun did not graduate.

Broun became a newspaper man in 1910 when he joined the *New York Morning Telegraph* writing baseball stories in the sports section. He was fired two years later after requesting a second raise in pay. He was then hired by the *New York Tribune*, where he worked from 1912 to 1921. Broun rose through the ranks at the *Tribune*, starting as a reporter and copy editor, was eventually promoted to drama critic, then book reviewer, and finally, columnist.

On June 7, 1917, Broun married novelist, political activist and future co-Round Tabler Ruth Hale. Together they had one son, Heywood Hale Broun, who the elder Broun would reference occasionally in his columns. Hale and Broun divorced in 1933, but remained amicable towards one another. In fact, Broun continued to live on the same property with Hale

109

after the divorce, until Hale unexpectedly died just under a year later.

In 1921, Broun joined the staff of the *New York World*, where his syndicated column *It Seems to Me* was begun. Originally, the column tended to focus on such genial fare as nature studies, but as Broun's sense of social justice began to emerge, the column turned to serious political discussion more often than not. Broun's belief that journalists could help right the country's social ills would lead him on crusades that endeared him to the underprivileged while enraging his employers.

In 1927, a highly politicized and controversial trial of two Italian immigrants charged with murder, known as the Sacco and Vanzetti case, culminated in the execution of the men. Some thought Sacco and Vanzetti guilty of the crime, but many famous socialists and intellectuals, including Dorothy Parker, Edna St. Vincent Millay, Bertrand Russell, and Heywood Broun considered the trial tantamount to a witch hunt. Broun used his column to attack the decision to execute so sharply that his editors requested that he write no more about the subject. To this, Broun responded by going on strike, refusing to write any more for the *New York World* until it printed two more columns he had prepared about the case. Broun won the fight and was persuaded to return. This return was short-lived, however, as Broun wrote a scathing retaliation against the *World* publishers in the news journal *The Nation*. He was fired as a consequence. Broun continued to write *It Seems to Me* for the Scripps-Howard newspapers, at first with the *New York World-Telegram*, then with the *New York Post*, in which the column ran until 1939.

Increasingly concerned with the social injustices he saw around him, such as racial discrimination and censorship,

110

Broun decided to champion his causes beyond the newspaper column. In 1930, he ran for Congress as a member of the Socialist party. His campaign was unsuccessful, but spawned the infamous slogan, "I'd rather be right than Roosevelt." Three years later, Broun was ejected from the Socialist Party after he appeared with members of the Communist Party at a political rally, demanding the release of the Scottsboro Nine.

In 1933, along with the editors of the *New York Evening Post*, the *New York Times* and the *New York Herald Tribune*, Broun established the American Newspaper Guild, which still operates today as the Newspaper Guild. Fittingly, the Newspaper Guild sponsors an annual Heywood Broun Award, given to a journalist for outstanding work, particularly that which helps correct an injustice.

Broun died of pneumonia at age 51 in Stamford, Connecticut. His funeral was held at St. Patrick's Cathedral in New York City, with more than 3,000 mourners present. Among those in attendance were New York City Mayor Fiorello La Guardia, actor-director George M. Cohan, columnist Walter Winchell, and actress Tallulah Bankhead. Broun is buried in the Cemetery of the Gate of Heaven in Hawthorne, New York.

PRIVATE OWNERSHIP OF OFFSPRING

Fannie Hurst gurgles with joy over the fact that her heroine in "Star Dust" is able to look over the whole tray of babies which is brought to her in the hospital and pick out her own. Miss Hurst attributes Lily's feat to "her mother instinct." A friend of ours, more practically minded than the novelist, suggests that she might have been aided by the fact that hospitals invariably place an identification tag around the neck of each child. For our part we have never been able to understand the fear of some parents about babies getting mixed up in the hospital. What difference does it make so long as you get a good one? Another's may be better than your own, and Lily, with a whole tray from which to choose, should not have made an instinctive clutch immediately for her own. It would have been rational for the lady in the story to have looked at them all before coming to any decision.

Of course, to tell the truth, there isn't much choice in the little ones. They need much more than necklaces with names on them to be persons. There really ought to be some system whereby small children after being born could be kept in the shop for a considerable period, like puppies, and not turned over to parents or guardians until in a condition more disciplined than usual. None of them amounts to much during the first year. We can't see, for the life of us, why your own should be any more interesting or precious to you during this time than the child of anybody else.

After two, of course, they are persons, but a parent must have a good deal of imagination if he can see much of himself in a child. Oh, yes, a nose or the eyes or the color of the hair or something like that, but the world is full of snub noses and brown eyes. To us it never seemed much more than a coincidence. And if it were something more, what of it? How can a man work up any inspiring sentimental gratification over the fact that after he is gone his nose will persist in the world? The hope of immortality through offspring offers no solace to us. The joys of being an ancestor are exaggerated.

Mind you, we do not mean for a moment to cry down the undeniable pleasure which arises from the privilege of being associated with a child of more than two years of age. For a person in rugged health who is not particularly dressed up and does not want to write a letter or read the newspaper, we can imagine few diversions more enjoyable than to have a child turned loose upon him. His own, if you wish, but only in the sense that it is the one to which he has become accustomed. The sense of paternity has nothing on earth to do with the fun. Only a person extraordinarily satisfied with himself can derive pleasure if this child in his house is a little person who gives him back nothing but a reflection. You want a new story and not the old one, which wasn't particularly satisfactory in the first place. We want Heywood Broun, 3rd, to start from scratch without having to lug along anything we have left him. As a matter of fact, we like him just as well as if he were no relation at all, because he seems to be a person quite different from what we might have expected. When he says he doesn't want to take a bath we feel abashed and wish we had been a cleaner child, but for the most part we find him leading his own life altogether. When he bends over the Victrola and plays the Siegfried Funeral March over and over again we have no feeling of guilt. We know we can't be blamed for that. He never got it from us.

And again, he is a person utterly strange, and therefore twice as interesting, when we find him standing up to people, us for instance, and saying that he won't do this or that because he doesn't want to. Much sharper than a serpent's tooth is the

113

pleasure of an abject parent who finds himself the father of a stubborn child. If the people from the hospital should suddenly call up tomorrow and say, "We find we've made a mistake. We sent the wrong child to you three years ago, but now we can exchange him and rectify everything," we would say, "No, this one's been around quite a while now and is giving approximate satisfaction, and if you don't mind you can keep the real one."

Plays and novels which picture meetings between fathers and sons parted from birth or before have always seemed singularly unconvincing to us. The old man says "My boy! My boy!" and weeps, and the young man looks him warmly in the eye and says, "There, there." Not a bit like it is our guess. If we had never seen H, 3rd, and had then met him at the end of twenty years, we wouldn't be particularly interested. Strangers always embarrass us. It would not even shock us much to find that they had sent him to Yale or that he brushed his hair straight back or wore spats. There are to us no ties at all just in being a father. A son is distinctly an acquired taste. It's the practice of parenthood that makes you feel that, after all, there may be something in it. And anybody's child will do for practice.

JACK THE GIANT KILLER

All the giants and most of the dragons were happy and contented folk. Neither fear nor shame was in them. They faced life squarely and liked it. And so they left no literature.

The business of writing was left to the dwarfs, who felt impelled to distort real values in order to make their own pitiful existence endurable. In their stories the little people earned ease of mind for themselves by making up yarns in which they killed giants, dragons and all the best people of the community who were too big and strong for them. Naturally, the giants and dragons merely laughed at such times as these highly drawn accounts of imaginary happenings were called to their attention.

But they laughed not only too soon but too long. Giants and dragons have died and the stories remain. The world believes today that St. George slew the dragon, and that Jack killed all those giants. The little man has imposed himself upon the world. Strength and size have come to be reproaches. The world has been won by the weak.

Undoubtedly, it is too late to do anything about this now. But there is a little dim and distant dragon blood in our veins. It boils when we hear the fairy stories and we remember the true version of Jack the Giant Killer, as it has been handed down by word of mouth in our family for a great many centuries. We can produce no tangible proofs, and we are willing to admit that the tale may have grown a little distorted here and there in the telling through the ages. Even so it sounds much more plausible to us than the one which has crept into the story books.

Jack was a Celt, a liar and a meager man. He had great green eyes and much practice in being pathetic. He could sing tenor and often did. But it was not in this manner that he lived. By trade he was a newspaper man though he called himself a journalist. In his shop there was a printing press and every afternoon he issued a newspaper which he called *Jack's Journal*. Under this name there ran the caption, "If you see it in *Jack's Journal* you may be sure that it actually occurred." Jack had no talent for brevity and little taste for truth. All in all he was a pretty poor newspaper man. We forgot to say that in addition to this he was exceedingly lazy. But he was a good liar.

This was the only thing which saved him. Day after day he would come to the office without a single item of local interest, and upon such occasions he made a practice of sitting down and making up something. Generally, it was far more thrilling than any of the real news of the community which clustered around one great highroad known as Main Street.

The town lay in a valley cupped between towering hills. On the hills, and beyond, lived the giants and the dragons, but there was little interchange between these fine people and the dwarfs of the village. Occasionally, a sliced drive from the giants' golf course would fall into the fields of the little people, who would ignorantly set down the great round object as a meteor from heaven. The giants were considerate as well as kindly and they made the territory of the little people out of bounds. Otherwise, an erratic golfer might easily have uprooted the first national bank, the Second Baptist Church, which stood next door, and *Jack's Journal* with one sweep of his niblick. If by any chance he failed to get out in one, the total destruction of mankind would have been imminent.

Once upon a time, a charitable dowager dragon sought to bring about a closer relationship between the peoples of the hills and the valley in spite of their difference in size. Hearing of a poor neglected family in the village, which was freezing to death because of want of coal, she leaned down from her mountain and breathed gently against the roof of the thatched cottage. Her intentions were excellent but the damage was $152,694, little of which was covered by insurance. After that the dragons and the giants decided to stop trying to do favors for the little people.

Being short of news one afternoon, Jack thought of the great gulf which existed between his reading public and the big fellows on the hill and decided that it would be safe to romance a little. Accordingly, he wrote a highly circumstantial story of the manner in which he had gone to the hills and killed a large giant with nothing more than his good broad sword. The story was not accepted as gospel by all the subscribers, but it was well told, and it argued an undreamed of power in the arm of man. People wanted to believe and accordingly they did. Encouraged, Jack began to kill dragons and giants with greater frequency in his newspaper. In fact, he called his last evening edition *The Five Star Giant Final* and never failed to feature a killing in it under great red block type.

The news of the Jack's doings came finally to the hill people and they were much amused, that is all but one giant called Fee Fi Fo Fum. The Fo Fums (pronounced Fohum) were one of the oldest families in the hills. Jack supposed that all the names he was using were fictitious, but by some mischance or other he happened one afternoon to use Fee Fi Fo Fum as the name of his current victim. The name was common enough and undoubtedly the thing was an accident, but Mr. Fo Fum did not see it in that light. To make it worse, Jack had gone on in his story with some stuff about captive princesses just for the sake

117

of sex appeal. Not only was Mr. Fo Fum an ardent Methodist, but his wife was jealous. There was a row in the Fo Fum home (see encyclopedia for Great Earthquake of 1007) and Fee swore revenge upon Jack.

"Make him print a retraction," said Mrs. Fo Fum.

"Retraction, nothing," roared Fee, "I'm going to eat up the presses."

Over the hills he went with giant strides and arrived at the office of *Jack's Journal* just at press time. Mr. Fo Fum was a little calmer by now, but still revengeful. He spoke to Jack in a whisper which shook the building, and told him that he purposed to step on him and bite his press in two.

"Wait until I have this last page made up," said Jack.

"Killing more giants, I presume?" said Fee with heavy satire.

"Bagged three this afternoon," said Jack. "Hero Slaughters Trio of Titans."

"My name is Fo Fum," said the giant. Jack did not recognize it because of the trick pronunciation and the visitor had to explain.

"I'm sorry," said Jack, "but if you've come for extra copies of the paper in which your name figures I can't give you any. The edition is exhausted."

Fo Fum spluttered and blew a bale of paper out of the window.

118

"Cut that out," said Jack severely. "All complaints must be made in writing. And while I'm about it you forgot to put your name down on one of those slips at the desk in the reception room. Don't forget to fill in that space about what business you want to discuss with the editor."

Fo Fum started to roar, but Jack's high and pathetic tenor cut through the great bass like a ship's siren in a storm.

"If you don't quit shaking this building I'll call Julius the office boy and have him throw you out."

"Take the air," added Jack severely, disregarding the fact that Fo Fum before entering the office had found it necessary to remove the roof. But now the giant was beginning to stoop a little. His face grew purple and he was swaying unsteadily on his feet.

"Hold on a minute," said Jack briskly, "don't go just yet. Stick around a second."

He turned to his secretary and dictated two letters of congratulation to distant emperors and another to a cardinal. "Tell the Pope," he said in conclusion, "that his conduct is admirable. Tell him I said so."

"Now, Mr. Fo Fum," said Jack turning back to the giant, "what I want from you is a picture. There is still plenty of light. I'll call up the staff photographer. The north meadow will give us room. Of course, you will have to be taken lying down because as far as the *Journal* goes you're dead. And just one thing more. Could you by any chance let me have one of your ears for our reception room?"

119

Fo Fum had been growing more and more purple, but now he toppled over with a crash, carrying part of the building with him. Almost two years before he had been warned by a doctor of apoplexy and sudden anger. Jack did not wait for the verdict of any medical examiner. He seized the speaking tube and shouted down to the composing room, "Jim, take out that old head. Make it read, 'Hero Finishes Four Ferocious Foemen.' And say, Jim, I want you to be ready to replate for a special extra with an eight column cut. I'll have the photographer here in a second. I killed that last giant right here in the office. Yes, and say, Jim, you'd better use that stock cut of me at the bottom of the page. A caption, let me see, put it in twenty-four point Cheltenham bold and make it read 'Jack—the Giant Killer.'"

ARE EDITORS PEOPLE?

One of the characters in "A Prince There Was" is the editor of a magazine and, curiously enough, he has been made the hero of the film. Of course, there may be something to be said for editors. Indeed, we have heard them trying to say it, and yet they remain among the forces of darkness and of mystery. By every rule of logic the editor in any story ought to be the villain.

It is not the darkness so much as the mystery which disturbs us. Only rarely have we been able to understand what an editor was talking about. Sometimes we have suspected that neither of us did. There was, for instance, the man who tapped upon his flat-topped desk and said with great precision and deliberation, "When you are writing for *Blank's Magazine,* you want to remember that *Blank's* is a magazine which is read at five o'clock in the afternoon."

He was our first editor. Disillusion had not yet set in. We still believed in Santa Claus and sanctums. And so we took home with us the advice about five o'clock and pondered. We remembered it perfectly, but that was not much good. *"Blank's* is a magazine which is read at five o'clock in the afternoon."* How were we to interpret this declaration of a principle? It was beyond our powers to write with ladyfingers. Possibly the editor meant that our style needed a little more lemon in it. There could be no complaint, we felt sure, against the sugar. Ten years of hard service on a New York morning newspaper had granulated us pretty thoroughly.

Having made up our mind that a slight increase in the acid content per column might enable us to qualify with the editor as a man who could write for five o'clock in the

121

afternoon, we were suddenly confronted with a new problem. *Blank's* was an international magazine. Did the editor mean five o'clock by London or San Francisco time? Until we knew the answer there was no good running our head against rejection slips. There was no way to tell whether he would like an essay entitled "On Pipe Smoking Before Breakfast in Surrey," or whether he would prefer a little something on "Is the Garden of Eden Mentioned in the Bible Actually California?" Naturally, if one were writing with San Francisco's five o'clock in mind he would go on to make some comparison between Los Angeles and the serpent.

After extended deliberation, we decided that perhaps it would be best not to try to write for *Blank's* at all. It might put a strain upon the versatility of a young man too hard for him to bear. Suppose, for instance, he worked faithfully and molded his style to meet all the demands and requirements of five o'clock in the afternoon, and then suppose just as he was in the middle of a long novel, daylight saving should be introduced? His art would then be exactly one hour off and he would be obliged to turn back his hands along with those of the clock.

Of course, even though you understand an editor you may not agree with him. The makers of magazines incline a little to dogma. Give a man a swivel chair and he will begin to lean back and tell you what the public wants. Gazing through his window over the throng of Broadway, a faraway look will come into his eyes and he will begin to speak very earnestly about the farmer in Iowa. The farmer in Iowa is enormously convenient to editors. He is as handy as a rejection slip. In refusing manuscripts which he doesn't want to take, an editor almost invariably blames it on some distant subscriber. "I like this very much myself," he will explain. "It's great stuff. I wish I could use it. That part about the bobbed hair is a scream. But none of it would mean anything to the farmer in Iowa. Won't you show me something again that isn't quite so sophisticated?"

Riding through Iowa, we always make it a point to shake our fist at the landscape. And if by any chance the train passes a farmer we try to hit him with some handy missile. And why not? He kept us out of print. At least they said he did.

And yet though editors are invariably doleful about the capacity of the farmer in Iowa and points west, it would be quite inaccurate to suggest any fundamental pessimism. An editor is always optimistic, particularly when a contributor asks for his check. But it really is a sincere and deep grained hopefulness. No editor could live from day to day without the faculty or arguing himself into the belief that the next number of his magazine is not going to be quite so bad as the last one.

Unfortunately he is not content to be a solitary tippler in good cheer. He feels that it is his duty to discover authors and inspirit them. Indeed, the average editor cannot escape feeling that telling a writer to do something is almost the same thing as performing it himself.

The editorial mind, so called, is afflicted with the King Cole complex. Types subject to this delusion are apt to believe that all they need do to get a thing is to call for it. You may remember that King Cole called for his bowl just as if there were no such thing as a Volstead amendment. "What we want is humor," says an editor, and he expects the unfortunate author to trot around the corner and come back with a quart of quips.

An editor would classify "What we want is humor" as a piece of cooperation on his part. It seems to him a perfect division of labor. After all, nothing remains for the author to do except to write.

Sometimes the mogul of a magazine will be even more specific. We confessed to an editor once that we were not very fertile in ideas, and he said, "Never mind, I'll think up something for you."

"Let me see," he continued, and crinkled his brow in that profound way which editors have. Suddenly the wrinkles vanished and his face lighted up. "That's it," he cried. "I want you to go and do us a series something like Mr. Dooley." He leaned back and fairly beamed satisfaction. He had done his best to make a humorist out of us. If failure followed it could only be because of shortsightedness and stubbornness on our part. We had our assignment.

Ruth Hale

1887–1934

"Thank God I am not cursed with the albatross of a sense of humor."

Ruth Hale was born in Rogersville, Tennessee to Richard and Anne Riley Hale. An extremely intelligent youth, Hale entered the Hollins Institute, now Hollins University, at the age of 13. After three years, she left to enroll in the Drexel Academy of Fine Art in Philadelphia where she studied painting and sculpture.

Despite her academic background in the visual arts, Hale found writing to be her first true passion. When she turned 18, she moved to Washington, D.C. and became a journalist writing for the Hearst syndicate. While working for the *Washington Post*, Hale became a much sought-after writer as well as socialite, even attending parties at the White House under Woodrow Wilson's presidency. Some years later, Hale moved back to Philadelphia and wrote a column for the *Philadelphia Public Ledger*, becoming one of the first widely-read female drama critics.

In another rare turn for women writers of her time, Hale wrote a few sports articles. This somewhat uncommon interest would play a part in her personal life a few years later. In 1915, Hale moved to New York City where she wrote features for *The New York Times*, *Vogue*, and *Vanity Fair*. Around this

125

time, she was introduced to well-known columnist and sportswriter Heywood Broun at a New York Giants baseball game. Hale and Brown hit it off, and after becoming fast friends with similar political leanings, married on June 6, 1917.

Already a trailblazer for women's roles in news writing, Hale would, through her marriage, continue to further her position as a strong women's activist. Hale did not adopt Broun's last name upon their wedding. In 1921, the two had plans to travel to Europe, and Hale requested a passport that bore her maiden name. Up to that point in time, the U.S. State Department had never issued a passport to a married woman not referred to by her husband's last name. Unable to be dissuaded, the government issued Hale a passport that read "Ruth Hale, also known as Mrs. Heywood Broun." She refused the passport, and both she and Broun cancelled their trip.

Later that year, Hale and Broun purchased a home in New York's Upper West Side. After navigating several legal hurdles, the couple had the deed to the property issued to both of them as separate people – not as a married couple. It is believed that Hale was the first married woman in New York history to have a deed issued in her own name. Hale was also founder and president of the Lucy Stone League, an organization that advocates for a woman's legal right to keep her last name upon marriage. The group's motto is "My name is the symbol for my identity and must not be lost."

In the late 1920's, Hale began to devote less time to journalism and more time to political activism. In addition to her involvement with the Lucy Stone League, she took, along with her husband, a leading role in protesting the executions of accused murderers Sacco and Vanzetti. The highly politicized campaign had a profound effect on Hale, and led her to the forefront of the fight against capital punishment.

While much of her time was spent championing political causes, Hale did continue to write into the 1930s, reviewing books for the *Brooklyn Eagle* and working as a theatrical press agent. She and Broun quietly and amicably divorced in November 1933, still living together on the same property in Connecticut. Just under a year later, Hale came down with severe intestinal flu at their home in Stamford. Broun rushed her to hospital in New York, but it was too late. Hale died on September 18 at age 47.

THE WOMAN'S PLACE

At last the women of this country are about to perform a great service – not one of those courtesy services about which so much is so volubly said and so little is done in repayment – but a good sturdy performance, that will probably bring these magnificent men folks right to their knees.

They are going to teach the unfortunates how to live under prohibitions and taboos. Of course there has never been any prodigality of freedom in this country – or any other – but what there was belonged to the men. The women had to take to the home and stay there. So the two sexes adjusted themselves to life with this difference, that the women had to do all the outwitting and circumventing, all the little smart twists and turns, all the cunning scheming by which people snatch off what they want without appearing to, whereas men got their much or little by prosily sticking their hands out for it.

This developed, naturally, not only somewhat diverse temperaments, but also greatly diverse equipments. When men cannot get what they want now by either asking or paying for it, they have no more resources. Bless them, they must return into the home, where the secret has been perfected for centuries on centuries of how to hoard a private stock and how to find a bootlegger. Under the steadily growing nonsenseorship regime, they are obliged to come and take lessons from the lately despised group of creatures to whom nonsenseorship is a well-thumbed story. If the world outside the home is to become as circumscribed and paternalized as the world inside it, obviously all the advantage lies with those who have been living under nonsenseorship long enough to have learned to manage it.

Thus woman moves over from her dull post as keeper of the virtues to the far more important and exciting post as keeper of the vices. It is not an ideal power which she thus acquires. But then none of this is about ideals. This is just a little practical study in what is going to happen, and why. Taboos never yet have added a cubit to the stature of the soul of humanity. They have nearly always been the chattering children of fear and pure idiocy. They have always tried to throw the race back on to all fours, and have left the nobility of standing upright wholly out of account.

The taboos which have surrounded women time out of mind have been so puerile and imbecile that one quite non-partisanly wonders why on earth they have been allowed to continue. A second thought demonstrates, of course, that fear has had the major part in it, and that skill in cheating has gone so far as practically to nullify the privations of the taboo.

But one must put by this hankering after nobility, and accept the plain fact that fear is the dominant human motive. What the race would do if fear were conquered, or at least faced sternly eye to eye, is staggering to contemplate. Perhaps God looks upon that vision. It may be that which gives Him patience. But man at best gives it one terrified squint in a lifetime. All behavior must take fear into account.

The man who lately brought back from the Amazon Basin news of a fear-dispelling drug used there by a savage tribe, would have been carried home from the steamer on the shoulders of his compatriots if for one moment he had been believed. His drug may do all he claimed for it, but a country which boasts a Volstead in full stride cannot force itself to take him seriously. The only likely part of his story was that the tribes who prepared the drug would put to instant death any woman who happened either to learn how to prepare it or did actually get some of it into her.

We recognize that part as familiar. We have made the same fight here against the fearless woman as the savages made on the Amazon. The only thing we were never smart enough to apply was the moral of the Kipling story about the two greatest armies in the world: the men who believed that they could not die till their time came, against those who wanted to die as soon as possible. It was from one or the other of these two kinds of fearlessness that women have trained themselves in wisdom.

This is the wisdom which moves them to secret laughter when they find their brothers in the throes of Volstead and Krafts. And it is from this wisdom that they will teach them all to be happy, though prohibited.

It is an unfortunate fact that humanity will not behave itself. It does not really warm to any of the current virtues. When the Eighteenth Amendment says it must not drink hard liquors, its inner heart's desire is to drink them, even beyond its normal and usual capacity. Prohibition is, it is true, one of the strikingly superimposed virtues. It has nothing whatever to recommend it in man's true feelings, and this is not true of many of the civilized traits, though probably not any of them meets with entire approval. We do think that before anything approaching a real art of living is perfected among us, the present ethical system will be wholly outmoded. Meanwhile, pressure brought to bear on the least welcome of all virtues is merely going to make bad behavior worse. But that is Volstead's business, not ours. Let him do battle with that octopus, while we bring up reinforcements to his enemies. Women know all about how to be bad and comfortable while the law goes on trying to make them good and otherwise. Just look at a few of the things on which they have cut their teeth.

We do not know, unfortunately, just at what point in her history woman went under the long siege of her taboos. Whether the system of keeping her publicly helpless and interdicted goes before church and state, or was the result of them, there is now no history to tell us. But certainly she always had one supreme power and one supreme weakness, and somewhere in time, her more neutrally equipped male companion played the one against her, to save his own skin from being stripped by the other.

But if the past is foggy, the present is not. We do know what is now, and has for a long time been, a shocking list of what she must not be allowed to do.

She cannot own and control her own property, for instance, except here and there in the world. Perhaps the theory was that she could not create property. But one would have said that such of it as she inherited she had as sound a right to as that that her brother inherited. But no such common sense notion prevailed. No matter how she came by it, it became her husband's as soon as she married. The law has always behaved as if a woman became a half-wit the moment she married. Seeing what she deliberately lost by it, perhaps the law is right. She lost control of her possessions, including herself. She lost her citizenship, and she lost her name, though this by custom and not by law. And finally, she never could acquire control even over her own children, which certainly she did create. We do not know how many of these disabilities would have been excused on the ground that they were for her own good. It seems likelier that they came under the head of that fine old abstraction, the general good. No longer back than 1914, H. G. Wells, in "Social Forces in England and America" observed that they would probably never be able to give women any real freedom because there were the children to consider. Mr. Wells did not appear to know that he was bridging a horrible conflict in terms with a pretty fatuity. Nor did he later give himself pause when, towards the end of the book, he complained that all the babies were being had by the low grade women, while the high grade ones were quite insensible to their duties.

It was possibly with an unruliness of this kind in contemplation that the law decided that women should know nothing of birth control. Now there's a taboo for you. Many of our very best people – the moral element, so called – will not even speak the words. But that prohibition, like all the others, has its side door – may one say its small-family entrance? The women who do not know all there is to know about it are just those poor, isolated, and ignorant women economically starved who should be the first to be told.

Consider the quaintest, we think, of all the proscriptions against women – that they cannot have citizenship in their own right. What is citizenship if it is not the assumption, made by the State, that because you were born within it, and had grown used to it and fond of it, and were attached to it by all the associations of blood ties, friendships, and what-not, you were therefore entitled to take part in it, and could be called on to give it service? If citizenship is a mere legal figment, by what right do States send their citizens to war? Yet women are theoretically transferred, body and bone, heart, memory, and soul, to whatever country or nation their husbands happen to give allegiance to. Isadora Duncan, born in California, of generations of Californians, and American all her life, has lately married a young Russian poet. Hereafter she must enter her country as an alien immigrant – if it so happens that the quota is not closed. Does anybody in his senses imagine that Isadora Duncan has been changed, or could be

132

changed, for better or worse? An opera singer who was in danger during the war of losing her position at the Metropolitan Opera House because she was an enemy alien, went forth and married an American. By that means she was actually supposed to have been made over into an American. Can naïveté go further?

For our present purposes we merely want to point out that what is done to one woman in the name of the public good is craftily used by the next one to serve her own ends. There is a terrifying proportion of women in America today who can vote, without knowing a word of our language, without participating in one particle of our common life, because their husbands have taken on American citizenship. They wouldn't be allowed to become American citizens if they wanted to, by any other means.

There are scores and scores of these legal absurdities conscripting the activities of women. Twenty books could be written about them, and probably will be. But we must leave them, with such representation as these few instances afford, and go from, the body of taboos that are done in the name of the good of the State, to that collection done for Woman's own personal good.

Some of these are legal and some are not, but they are all operative. They are all things she has to go around, or under. She cannot serve on juries. She is always righteously barred from courtrooms when there is to be testimony concerning sex. Woman, the mother of children, the realist of sex compared to whom the most sympathetic of males is at best an outsider, is to be "protected" from a few scandalous narratives. Of course all women know that they are barred from juries not because the happenings in court would shock or even surprise them, but because they would embarrass their far more sensitive and finicky men. So what they wish to know of court proceedings, they learn from their good men, in the pleasant privacy of their homes. If the juries are so much the worse for this sort of thing, and they are, the matter cannot be helped by the ladies, dear knows, and the men would die almost any death other than that of ravaged modesty.

Probably the most ungrateful of the restrictions on females is that forbidding them to hold office in churches. This has been put on all sorts of high grounds, chief among them being that women could do so much abler work in little auxiliaries of their own. This contention was challenged about two years ago in the House of Commons, by Maud Royden, the English Lay Evangelist to whom the pulpits of London are forbidden, with one or two exceptions. Miss Royden, whose preaching was being bitterly opposed by several members of the House, annoyed them all considerably by saying that the Church of England had already had two women as its absolute head. This was denied in a great sputter, to which Miss Royden replied, "How about Queen Elizabeth and Queen Victoria?" Well, this happened to be something that nobody could gainsay, but into the wrathy silence which followed, one member of the House rose to his feet and let the cat right out of the bag. If women were given church authority, he said, they would refuse to accept their husbands' authority in their homes, and England would go to rack and ruin. This is one of the few recorded occasions when a taboo-er so far forgot himself, and American church potentates do not like to be reminded of it. Within a month, one of the Protestant sects in this country has given women the right to hold minor offices, but three others, in general convention, refused even to consider it.

Again we are going to rest our case on selected instances, and return to a consideration of how these walled-in women have learned to live comfortably and with some self-

134

respect behind the garrison wall. It is this, after all, which they must now teach their men.

The first thing that happened to the woman who married was that she became legally non-existent. But though she was scratched off the public books, she couldn't exactly be scratched out of her husband's scheme of general well-being. Neither could the race make great strides without her. After everything in the world had been done to make her as harmless as possible, she still remained non-ignorable. Two courses were open to her; and she has always used whichever of the two was necessary at the time. She could be so sweet and beguiling, so full of blandishments, that man rushed out to bring her all and more than she had been prohibited from having. Or she could terrify him, both by her temper and her biological superiority, into stopping his entire precious machinery against her, and thanking his stars that he could get off with a whole skin.

Of course these things have not always worked out just so. There have been the tragic mischances. But in the main, an oppressed people learn how to out-smile or out-snarl the oppressor. The Eighteenth Amendment may yet live to wish it was dead. Mr. Volstead seems to have believed that the nonsenseorship game was new and exciting, and could be trusted to carry itself by storm. Not while the ancient wisdom of long-borne bans and communicadoes looked out of the female eye. There was a body of experts in existence of whom, apparently, he had never even heard.

He never once thought how the twentieth century was to become known as the Century of The Home, with the home brew, and the subscription editions, and the sagacities of women. If he should complain that there is no honor and fine living in all of this, we shall have to agree with him. But we

135

can answer that by guile we have preserved our joys, and cleared our way out from the shadows of his big totem pole. If we have but little magnificence, we have as much as anybody can ever have who is hounded by the legal virtues. And if we may keep a little gaiety for life, by that much do we make him bite the dust. It isn't pretty, but it's art.

Edna Ferber

1885–1968

"Living in the past is a dull and lonely business; looking back strains the neck muscles, causing you to bump into people not going your way."

Novelist and playwright Edna Ferber was born in Kalamazoo, Michigan, to Hungarian-born shop owner Jacob Ferber and his wife Julia, a native of Milwaukee, Wisconsin. The family lived all over the Midwest during Edna's childhood, finally settling in Appleton, Wisconsin when Edna was 12. Her talents as a writer emerged early when she became editor of her high school newspaper, the *Ryan Clarion*. Upon graduation at age 17, her senior essay so impressed the editor of the *Appleton Daily Crescent* that she was offered a job as a reporter for the paper at $3.00 an hour. Ferber's modest family income prompted her to accept the job instead of pursuing her original dream to become a stage actress.

Ferber went on to write for the *Milwaukee Journal* once her job at the *Crescent* ended. While there, a bout with anemia, coupled with her extreme work ethic, caused her to collapse. During her recovery period, Ferber wrote her first short story, *The Homely Heroine*, and began her first novel, *Dawn O'Hara*. *The Homely Heroine* was published in 1910, with her novel published soon after in 1911, thus jump-starting her very prolific career as a writer.

Ferber first gained literary fame with a series of short stories about the adventures of Emma McChesney, a traveling underskirt saleswoman. There were thirty McChesney stories in all, published in national magazines and exceedingly popular with the reading public. With collaborator and fellow Round Table member George S. Kaufman, Ferber wrote several critically acclaimed plays. These included *The Royal Family*, *Dinner at Eight*, and *Stage Door*, which was later adapted into the movie of the same name, starring Katherine Hepburn and Ginger Rogers. The movie's storyline bore so little resemblance to the play's, however, that Kaufman joked the film should've been called "Screen Door."

Several more theatrical and film adaptations were made based on Ferber's works, including *Show Boat*, *Giant*, *Ice Palace*, *Saratoga Trunk*, *Cimarron*, and *So Big*, which originally garnered the author a Pulitzer Prize. These adaptations seemed almost a natural progression, as Ferber's style was one of vividly imagined scene and expansive plot, and could easily be transformed to a visual medium. What stands out as her signature, however, is her unmatched skill in character development.

Perhaps because of her Midwest upbringing, Ferber had always been a champion of "regular folk." It was the non-glamorous, seemingly ordinary people whom she believed had the most character, and it was this population she heralded in her work. Strong female protagonists were almost always a constant, as were those who faced and fought discrimination in one way or another.

Edna Ferber wrote over thirty novels, plays, and short story collections, as well as two autobiographies, *A Peculiar Treasure* and *A Kind of Magic*, before her death at age 82 of stomach cancer. Never married and never having had children, Ferber seemed to view her works with both a cynical and a maternal eye.   In the foreword to her short story collection *Buttered Side Down*, she writes:

> *"And so," the story writers used to say, "they lived happily ever after."*

> *Um-m-m... maybe.   After the glamour had worn off, and the glass slippers were worn out, did the Prince never find Cinderella's manner redolent of the kitchen hearth; and was it never necessary that he remind her to be more careful of her finger-nails and grammar?   After Puss in Boots had won wealth and a wife for his young master did not that gentleman often fume with chagrin because the neighbors, perhaps, refused to call on the lady of the former poor miller's son?*

> *It is a great risk to take with one's book-children. These stories make no such promises.   They stop just short of the phrase of the old story writers, and end truthfully, thus: And so they lived.*

THE KITCHEN SIDE OF THE DOOR

The City was celebrating New Year's Eve. Spelled thus, with a capital C, know it can mean but New York. In the Pink Fountain room of the Newest Hotel all those grand old forms and customs handed down to us for the occasion were being rigidly observed in all their original quaintness. The Van Dyked man who looked like a Russian Grand Duke (he really was a chiropodist) had drunk champagne out of the pink satin slipper of the lady who behaved like an actress (she was forelady at Schmaus' Wholesale Millinery, eighth floor). The two respectable married ladies there in the corner had been kissed by each other's husbands. The slim, Puritan-faced woman in white, with her black hair so demurely parted and coiled in a sleek knot, had risen suddenly from her place and walked indolently to the edge of the splashing pink fountain in the center of the room, had stood contemplating its shallows with a dreamy half-smile on her lips, and then had lifted her slim legs slowly and gracefully over its fern-fringed basin and had waded into its chilling midst, trailing her exquisite white satin and chiffon draperies after her, and scaring the goldfish into fits. The loudest scream of approbation had come from the yellow-haired, loose-lipped youth who had made the wager, and lost it. The heavy blonde in the inevitable violet draperies showed signs of wanting to dance on the table. Her companion – a structure made up of layer upon layer, and fold upon fold of flabby tissue – knew all the waiters by their right names, and insisted on singing with the orchestra and beating time with a rye roll. The clatter of dishes was giving way to the clink of glasses.

In the big, bright kitchen back of the Pink Fountain room, Miss Gussie Fink sat at her desk, calm, watchful, insolent-eyed, a goddess sitting in judgment. On the pay roll of

140

the Newest Hotel Miss Gussie Fink's name appeared as kitchen checker, but her regular job was goddessing. Her altar was a high desk in a corner of the busy kitchen, and it was an altar of incense, of burnt-offerings, and of showbread. Inexorable as a goddess of the ancients was Miss Fink, and ten times as difficult to appease. For this is the rule of the Newest Hotel, that no waiter may carry his laden tray restaurantward until its contents have been viewed and duly checked by the eye and hand of Miss Gussie Fink, or her assistants. Flat upon the table must go every tray, off must go each silver dish-cover, lifted must be each napkin to disclose its treasure of steaming corn or hot rolls. Clouds of incense rose before Miss Gussie Fink and she sniffed it unmoved, her eyes, beneath level brows, regarding savory broiler or cunning ice with equal indifference, appraising alike lobster cocktail or onion soup, traveling from blue points to brie. Things a la and things glace were all one to her. Gazing at food was Miss Gussie Fink's occupation, and just to see the way she regarded a boneless squab made you certain that she never ate.

In spite of the I-don't-know-how-many (see ads) New Year's Eve diners for whom food was provided that night, the big, busy kitchen was the most orderly, shining, spotless place imaginable. But Miss Gussie Fink was the neatest, most immaculate object in all that great, clean room. There was that about her which suggested daisies in a field, if you know what I mean. This may have been due to the fact that her eyes were brown while her hair was gold, or it may have been something about the way her collars fitted high, and tight, and smooth, or the way her close white sleeves came down to meet her pretty hands, or the way her shining hair sprang from her forehead. Also the smooth creaminess of her clear skin may have had something to do with it. But privately, I think it was due to the way she wore her shirtwaists. Miss Gussie Fink could wear a starched white shirtwaist under a close-fitting winter coat,

141

remove the coat, run her right forefinger along her collar's edge and her left thumb along the back of her belt and disclose to the admiring world a blouse as unwrinkled and unsullied as though it had just come from her own skilful hands at the ironing board. Miss Gussie Fink was so innately, flagrantly, beautifully clean-looking that – well, there must be a stop to this description.

She was the kind of girl you'd like to see behind the counter of your favorite delicatessen, knowing that you need not shudder as her fingers touch your Sunday night supper slices of tongue, and Swiss cheese, and ham. No girl had ever dreamed of refusing to allow Gussie to borrow her chamois for a second.

Tonight Miss Fink had come on at 10 P.M., which was just two hours later than usual. She knew that she was to work until 6 A.M., which may have accounted for the fact that she displayed very little of what the fans call ginger as she removed her hat and coat and hung them on the hook behind the desk. The prospect of that all-night, eight-hour stretch may have accounted for it, I say. But privately, and entre nous, it didn't. For here you must know of Heiny. Heiny, alas! Now Henri.

Until two weeks ago Henri had been Heiny and Miss Fink had been Kid. When Henri had been Heiny he had worked in the kitchen at many things, but always with a loving eye on Miss Gussie Fink. Then one wild night there had been a waiters' strike – wages or hours or tips or all three. In the confusion that followed Heiny had been pressed into service and a chopped coat. He had fitted into both with unbelievable nicety, proving that waiters are born, not made. Those little tricks and foibles that are characteristic of the genus waiter seemed to envelop him as though a fairy garment had fallen upon his shoulders. The folded napkin under his left arm seemed to have been placed there by nature, so perfectly did it fit into place. The ghostly tread, the little whisking skip, the half-simper, the deferential bend that had in it at the same time something of insolence, all were there; the very "Yes, miss," and "Very good, sir," rose automatically and correctly to his untrained lips. Cinderella rising resplendent from her ash-strewn hearth was not more completely transformed than Heiny in his role of Henri. And with the transformation Miss Gussie Fink had been left behind her desk disconsolate.

Kitchens are as quick to seize upon these things and gossip about them as drawing rooms are. And because Miss Gussie Fink had always worn a little air of aloofness to all except Heiny, the kitchen was the more eager to make the most of its morsel. Each turned it over under his tongue – Tony, the Crook, whom Miss Fink had scorned; Francois, the entree cook, who often forgot he was married; Miss Sweeney, the bar-checker, who was jealous of Miss Fink's complexion. Miss Fink heard, and said nothing. She only knew that there would be no dear figure waiting for her when the night's work was done. For two weeks now she had put on her hat and coat and gone her way at one o'clock alone. She discovered that to be taken home night after night under Heiny's tender escort had taught her a ridiculous terror of the streets at night now that she was without protection. Always the short walk from the car to the flat where Miss Fink lived with her mother had been a glorious, star-lit, all too brief moment. Now it was an endless and terrifying trial, a thing of shivers and dread, fraught with horror of passing the alley just back of Cassidey's buffet. There had even been certain little half-serious, half-jesting talks about the future into which there had entered the subject of a little delicatessen and restaurant in a desirable neighborhood, with Heiny in the kitchen, and a certain blonde,

143

neat, white-shirtwaisted person in charge of the desk and front shop.

She and her mother had always gone through a little formula upon Miss Fink's return from work. They never used it now. Gussie's mother was a real mother – the kind that wakes up when you come home.

"That you, Gussie?" Ma Fink would call from the bedroom, at the sound of the key in the lock.

"It's me, ma."

"Heiny bring you home?"

"Sure," happily.

"There's a bit of sausage left, and some pie if – "

"Oh, I ain't hungry. We stopped at Joey's downtown and had a cup of coffee and a ham on rye. Did you remember to put out the milk bottle?"

For two weeks there had been none of that. Gussie had learned to creep silently into bed, and her mother, being a mother, feigned sleep.

Tonight at her desk Miss Gussie Fink seemed a shade cooler, more self-contained, and daisylike than ever. From somewhere at the back of her head she could see that Heiny was avoiding her desk and was using the services of the checker at the other end of the room. And even as the poison of this was eating into her heart she was tapping her forefinger imperatively on the desk before her and saying to Tony, the Crook:

"Down on the table with that tray, Tony – flat. This may be a busy little New Year's Eve, but you can't come any of your sleight-of-hand stuff on me." For Tony had a little trick of concealing a dollar-and-a-quarter sirloin by the simple method of slapping the platter close to the underside of his tray and holding it there with long, lean fingers outspread, the entire bit of knavery being concealed in the folds of a flowing white napkin in the hand that balanced the tray. Into Tony's eyes there came a baleful gleam. His lean jaw jutted out threateningly.

"You're the real Weissenheimer kid, ain't you?" he sneered. "Never mind. I'll get you at recess."

"Some day," drawled Miss Fink, checking the steak, "the house'll get wise to your stuff and then you'll have to go back to the coal wagon. I know so much about you it's beginning to make me uncomfortable. I hate to carry around a burden of crime."

"You're a sorehead because Heiny turned you down and now – "

"Move on there!" snapped Miss Fink, "or I'll call the steward to settle you. Maybe he'd be interested to know that you've been counting in the date and your waiter's number, and adding 'em in at the bottom of your check."

Tony, the Crook, turned and skimmed away toward the dining-room, but the taste of victory was bitter in Miss Fink's mouth.

Midnight struck. There came from the direction of the Pink Fountain Room a clamor and din which penetrated the

145

thickness of the padded doors that separated the dining-room from the kitchen beyond. The sound rose and swelled above the blare of the orchestra. Chairs scraped on the marble floor as hundreds rose to their feet. The sound of clinking glasses became as the jangling of a hundred bells. There came the sharp spat of hand-clapping, then cheers, yells, huzzas. Through the swinging doors at the end of the long passageway Miss Fink could catch glimpses of dazzling color, of shimmering gowns, of bare arms uplifted, of flowers, and plumes, and jewels, with the rosy light of the famed pink fountain casting a gracious glow over all. Once she saw a tall young fellow throw his arm about the shoulder of a glorious creature at the next table, and though the door swung shut before she could see it, Miss Fink knew that he had kissed her.

There were no New Year's greetings in the kitchen back of the Pink Fountain Room. It was the busiest moment in all that busy night. The heat of the ovens was so intense that it could be felt as far as Miss Fink's remote corner. The swinging doors between dining-room and kitchen were never still. A steady stream of waiters made for the steam tables before which the white-clad chefs stood ladling, carving, basting, serving, gave their orders, received them, stopped at the checking-desk, and sped dining-roomward again. Tony, the Crook, was cursing at one of the little Polish vegetable girls who had not been quick enough about the garnishing of a salad, and she was saying, over and over again, in her thick tongue:

"Aw, shod op yur mout'!"

The thud-thud of Miss Fink's checking-stamp kept time to flying footsteps, but even as her practiced eye swept over the tray before her she saw the steward direct Henri toward her desk, just as he was about to head in the direction of the minor checking-desk. Beneath downcast lids she saw him coming. There was about Henri tonight a certain radiance, a sort of electrical elasticity, so nimble, so tireless, so exuberant was he. In the eyes of Miss Gussie Fink he looked heartbreakingly handsome in his waiter's uniform – handsome, distinguished, remote, and infinitely desirable. And just behind him, revenge in his eye, came Tony.

The flat surface of the desk received Henri's tray. Miss Fink regarded it with a cold and business-like stare. Henri whipped his napkin from under his left arm and began to remove covers, dexterously. Off came the first silver, dome-shaped top.

"Guinea hen," said Henri.

"I seen her lookin' at you when you served the little necks," came from
Tony, as though continuing a conversation begun in some past moment of pause, "and she's some lovely doll, believe me."

Miss Fink scanned the guinea hen thoroughly, but with a detached air, and selected the proper stamp from the box at her elbow. Thump! On the broad pasteboard sheet before her appeared the figures $1.75 after
Henri's number.

"Think so?" grinned Henri, and removed another cover. "One candied sweets."

"I bet some day we'll see you in the Sunday papers, Heiny," went on Tony, "with a piece about handsome waiter runnin' away with beautiful s'ciety girl. Say; you're too perfect even for a waiter."

Thump! Thirty cents.

147

"Quit your kiddin'," said the flattered Henri. "One endive, French dressing."

Thump! "Next!" said Miss Fink, dispassionately, yawned, and smiled fleetingly at the entree cook who wasn't looking her way. Then, as Tony slid his tray toward her: "How's business, Tony? H'm? How many two-bit cigar bands have you slipped onto your own private collection of nickel straights and made a twenty-cent rake-off?"

But there was a mist in the bright brown eyes as Tony the Crook turned away with his tray. In spite of the satisfaction of having had the last word, Miss Fink knew in her heart that Tony had "got her at recess," as he had said he would.

Things were slowing up for Miss Fink. The stream of hurrying waiters was turned in the direction of the kitchen bar now. From now on the eating would be light, and the drinking heavy. Miss Fink, with time hanging heavy, found herself blinking down at the figures stamped on the pasteboard sheet before her, and in spite of the blinking, two marks that never were intended for a checker's report splashed down just over the $1.75 after Henri's number. A lovely doll! And she had gazed at Heiny. Well, that was to be expected. No woman could gaze unmoved upon Heiny. "A lovely doll... "

"Hi, Miss Fink!" it was the steward's voice. "We need you over in the bar to help Miss Sweeney check the drinks. They're coming too swift for her. The eating will be light from now on; just a little something salty now and then."

So Miss Fink dabbed covertly at her eyes and betook herself out of the atmosphere of roasting, and broiling, and frying, and stewing; away from the sight of great copper kettles, and glowing coals and hissing pans, into a little world fragrant with mint, breathing of orange and lemon peel, perfumed with pineapple, redolent of cinnamon and clove, reeking with things spirituous. Here the splutter of the broiler was replaced by the hiss of the siphon, and the pop-pop of corks, and the tinkle and clink of ice against glass.

"Hello, dearie!" cooed Miss Sweeney, in greeting, staring hard at the suspicious redness around Miss Fink's eyelids. "Ain't you sweet to come over here in the headache department and help me out! Here's the wine list. You'll prob'ly need it. Say, who do you suppose invented New Year's Eve? They must've had a imagination like a Greek bus boy. I'm limp as a rag now, and it's only two-thirty. I've got a regular cramp in my wrist from checkin' quarts. Say, did you hear about Heiny's crowd?"

"No," said Miss Fink, evenly, and began to study the first page of the wine list under the heading "Champagnes of Noted Vintages."

"Well," went on Miss Sweeney's little thin, malicious voice, "he's fell in soft. There's a table of three, and they're drinkin' 1874 Imperial Crown at twelve dollars per, like it was Waukesha ale. And every time they finish a bottle one of the guys pays for it with a brand new ten and a brand new five and tells Heiny to keep the change. Can you beat it?"

"I hope," said Miss Fink, pleasantly, "that the supply of 1874 will hold out till morning. I'd hate to see them have to come down to ten dollar wine. Here you, Tony! Come back here! I may be a new hand in this department but I'm not so green that you can put a gold label over on me as a yellow label. Notice that I'm checking you another fifty cents."

"Ain't he the grafter!" laughed Miss Sweeney. She leaned toward Miss
Fink and lowered her voice discreetly. "Though I'll say this for'm. If you let him get away with it now an' then, he'll split even with you. H'm? Oh, well, now, don't get so high and mighty. The management expects it in this department. That's why they pay starvation wages."

An unusual note of color crept into Miss Gussie Fink's smooth cheek. It deepened and glowed as Heiny darted around the corner and up to the bar. There was about him an air of suppressed excitement – suppressed, because Heiny was too perfect a waiter to display emotion.

"Not another!" chanted the bartenders, in chorus.

"Yes," answered Henri, solemnly, and waited while the wine cellar was made to relinquish another rare jewel.

"Oh, you Heiny!" called Miss Sweeney, "tell us what she looks like. If I had time I'd take a peek myself. From what Tony says she must look something like Maxine Elliot, only brighter."

Henri turned. He saw Miss Fink. A curious little expression came into his eyes – a Heiny look, it might have been called, as he regarded his erstwhile sweetheart's unruffled attire, and clear skin, and steady eye and glossy hair. She was looking past him in that baffling, maddening way that angry women have. Some of Henri's poise seemed to desert him in that moment. He appeared a shade less debonair as he received the precious bottle from the wine man's hands. He made for Miss Fink's desk and stood watching her while she checked his order. At the door he turned and looked over his shoulder at Miss Sweeney.

150

"Some time," he said, deliberately, "when there's no ladies around, I'll tell you what I think she looks like."

And the little glow of color in Miss Gussie Fink's smooth cheek became a crimson flood that swept from brow to throat.

"Oh, well," snickered Miss Sweeney, to hide her own discomfiture, "this is little Heiny's first New Year's Eve in the dining-room. Honest, I b'lieve he's shocked. He don't realize that celebratin' New Year's Eve is like eatin' oranges. You got to let go your dignity t' really enjoy 'em."

Three times more did Henri enter and demand a bottle of the famous vintage, and each time he seemed a shade less buoyant. His elation diminished as his tips grew greater until, as he drew up at the bar at six o'clock, he seemed wrapped in impenetrable gloom.

"Them hawgs sousin' yet?" shrilled Miss Sweeney. She and Miss Fink had climbed down from their high stools, and were preparing to leave. Henri nodded, drearily, and disappeared in the direction of the Pink Fountain Room.

Miss Fink walked back to her own desk in the corner near the dining room door. She took her hat off the hook, and stood regarding it, thoughtfully. Then, with a little air of decision, she turned and walked swiftly down the passageway that separated dining-room from kitchen. Tillie, the scrub-woman, was down on her hands and knees in one corner of the passage. She was one of a small army of cleaners that had begun the work of clearing away the debris of the long night's revel. Miss Fink lifted her neat skirts high as she tip-toed through the little soapy pool that followed in the wake of Tillie, the scrub-woman. She opened the swinging doors a cautious

151

little crack and peered in. What she saw was not pretty. If the words sordid and bacchanalian had been part of Miss Fink's vocabulary they would have risen to her lips then. The crowd had gone. The great room contained not more than half a dozen people. Confetti littered the floor. Here and there a napkin, crushed and bedraggled into an unrecognizable ball, lay under a table. From an overturned bottle the dregs were dripping drearily. The air was stale, stifling, poisonous.

At a little table in the center of the room Henri's three were still drinking. They were doing it in a dreadful and businesslike way. There were two men and one woman. The faces of all three were mahogany colored and expressionless. There was about them an awful sort of stillness. Something in the sight seemed to sicken Gussie Fink. It came to her that the wintry air outdoors must be gloriously sweet, and cool, and clean in contrast to this. She was about to turn away, with a last look at Heiny yawning behind his hand, when suddenly the woman rose unsteadily to her feet, balancing herself with her finger tips on the table. She raised her head and stared across the room with dull, unseeing eyes, and licked her lips with her tongue. Then she turned and walked half a dozen paces, screamed once with horrible shrillness, and crashed to the floor. She lay there in a still, crumpled heap, the folds of her exquisite gown rippling to meet a little stale pool of wine that had splashed from some broken glass. Then this happened. Three people ran toward the woman on the floor, and two people ran past her and out of the room. The two who ran away were the men with whom she had been drinking, and they were not seen again. The three who ran toward her were Henri, the waiter, Miss Gussie Fink, checker, and Tillie, the scrub-woman. Henri and Miss Fink reached her first. Tillie, the scrub-woman, was a close third. Miss Gussie Fink made as though to slip her arm under the poor bruised head, but Henri caught her wrist fiercely (for a waiter) and pulled her to her feet almost roughly.

"You leave her alone, Kid," he commanded.

Miss Gussie Fink stared, indignation choking her utterance. And as she stared the fierce light in Henri's eyes was replaced by the light of tenderness.

"We'll tend to her," said Henri; "she ain't fit for you to touch. I wouldn't let you soil your hands on such truck." And while Gussie still stared he grasped the unconscious woman by the shoulders, while another waiter grasped her ankles, with Tillie, the scrub-woman, arranging her draperies pityingly around her, and together they carried her out of the dining-room to a room beyond.

Back in the kitchen Miss Gussie Fink was preparing to don her hat, but she was experiencing some difficulty because of the way in which her fingers persisted in trembling. Her face was turned away from the swinging doors, but she knew when Henri came in. He stood just behind her, in silence. When she turned to face him she found Henri looking at her, and as he looked all the Heiny in him came to the surface and shone in his eyes. He looked long and silently at Miss Gussie Fink – at the sane, simple, wholesomeness of her, at her clear brown eyes, at her white forehead from which the shining hair sprang away in such a delicate line, at her immaculately white shirtwaist, and her smooth, snug-fitting collar that came up to the lobes of her little pink ears, at her creamy skin, at her trim belt. He looked as one who would rest his eyes – eyes weary of gazing upon satins, and jewels, and rouge, and carmine, and white arms, and bosoms.

"Gee, Kid! You look good to me," he said.

"Do I – Heiny?" whispered Miss Fink.

"Believe me!" replied Heiny, fervently. "It was just a case of swelled head. Forget it, will you? Say, that gang in there tonight – why, say, that gang..."

"I know," interrupted Miss Fink.

"Going home?" asked Heiny.

"Yes."

"Suppose we have a bite of something to eat first," suggested Heiny.

Miss Fink glanced round the great, deserted kitchen. As she gazed a little expression of disgust wrinkled her pretty nose – the nose that perforce had sniffed the scent of so many rare and exquisite dishes.

"Sure," she assented, joyously, "but not here. Let's go around the corner to Joey's. I could get real chummy with a cup of good hot coffee and a ham on rye."

He helped her on with her coat, and if his hands rested a moment on her shoulders who was there to see it? A few sleepy, wan-eyed waiters and Tillie, the scrub-woman. Together they started toward the door. Tillie, the scrubwoman, had worked her wet way out of the passage and into the kitchen proper. She and her pail blocked their way. She was sopping up a soapy pool with an all-encompassing gray scrub-rag. Heiny and Gussie stopped a moment perforce to watch her. It was rather fascinating to see how that artful scrub-rag craftily closed in upon the soapy pool until it engulfed it. Tillie sat

154

back on her knees to wring out the water-soaked rag. There was something pleasing in the sight. Tillie's blue calico was faded white in patches and at the knees it was dark with soapy water. Her shoes were turned up ludicrously at the toes, as scrub-women's shoes always are. Tillie's thin hair was wadded back into a moist knob at the back and skewered with a gray-black hairpin. From her parboiled, shriveled fingers to her ruddy, perspiring face there was nothing of grace or beauty about Tillie. And yet Heiny found something pleasing there. He could not have told you why, so how can I, unless to say that it was, perhaps, for much the same reason that we rejoice in the wholesome, safe, reassuring feel of the gray woolen blanket on our bed when we wake from a horrid dream.

"A Happy New Year to you," said Heiny gravely, and took his hand out of his pocket.

Tillie's moist right hand closed over something. She smiled so that one saw all her broken black teeth.

"The same t' you," said Tillie. "The same t' you."

GIGOLO

In the first place, *gigolo* is slang. In the second place (with no desire to appear patronizing, but one's French conversation class does not include the *argot*), it is French slang. In the third place, the gig is pronounced "zhig," and the whole is not a respectable word. Finally, it is a term of utter contempt.

A gigolo, generally speaking, is a man who lives off women's money. In the mad year 1922 A.W., a gigolo, definitely speaking, designated one of those incredible and pathetic male creatures, born of the war, who, for ten francs or more or even less, would dance with any woman wishing to dance on the crowded floors of public tea rooms, dinner or supper rooms in the cafes, hotels, and restaurants of France. Lean, sallow, handsome, expert, and unwholesome, one saw them everywhere, their slim waists and sleek heads in juxtaposition to plump, respectable American matrons and slender, respectable American flappers. For that matter, feminine respectability of almost every nationality (except the French) yielded itself to the skilful guidance of the genus gigolo in the tango or fox-trot. Naturally, no decent French girl would have been allowed for a single moment to dance with a gigolo. But America, touring Europe like mad after years of enforced absence, outnumbered all other nations atravel ten to one.

By no feat of fancy could one imagine Gideon Gory, of the Winnebago, Wisconsin, Gorys, employed daily and nightly as a gigolo in the gilt and marble restaurants that try to out-sparkle the Mediterranean along the Promenade des Anglais in Nice. Gideon Gory, of Winnebago, Wisconsin! Why, any one knows that the Gorys were to Winnebago what the Romanoffs were to Russia — royal, remote, omnipotent. Yet the Romanoffs went in the cataclysm, and so, too, did the Gorys. To appreciate the depths to which the boy Gideon had fallen one must have known the Gorys in their glory. It happened something like this:

The Gorys lived for years in the great, ugly, sprawling, luxurious old frame house on Cass Street. It was high up on the bluff overlooking the Fox River and, incidentally, the huge pulp and paper mills across the river in which the Gory money had been made. The Gorys were so rich and influential (for Winnebago, Wisconsin) that they didn't bother to tear down the old frame house and build a stone one, or to cover its faded front with cosmetics of stucco. In most things the Gorys led where Winnebago could not follow. They disdained to follow where Winnebago led. The Gorys had an automobile when those vehicles were entered from the rear and when Winnebago roads were a wallow of mud in the spring and fall and a snow-lined trench in the winter. The family was of the town, and yet apart from it. The Gorys knew about golf, and played it in far foreign playgrounds when the rest of us thought of it, if we thought of it at all, as something vaguely Scotch, like haggis. They had oriental rugs and hardwood floors when the town still stepped on carpets; and by the time the rest of the town had caught up on rugs the Gorys had gone back to carpets, neutral tinted. They had fireplaces in bedrooms, and used them, like characters in an English novel. Old Madame Gory had a slim patent leather foot, with a buckle, and carried a sunshade when she visited the flowers in the garden. Old Gideon was rumoured to have wine with his dinner. Gideon Junior (father of Giddy) smoked cigarettes with his monogram on them. Shroeder's grocery ordered endive for them, all blanched and delicate in a wicker basket from France or Belgium, when we had just become accustomed to head lettuce.

Every prosperous small American town has its Gory family. Every small town newspaper relishes the savoury tid-bits that fall from the rich table of the family life. Thus you saw that Mr. and Mrs. Gideon Gory, Jr., have returned from California where Mr. Gory had gone for the polo. Mr. and Mrs. Gideon Gory, Jr., announce the birth, in New York, of a son, Gideon III (our, in a manner of speaking, hero). Mr. and Mrs. Gideon Gory, Jr., and son Gideon III, left today for England and the continent. It is understood that Gideon III will be placed at school in England. Mr. and Mrs. Gideon Gory, accompanied by Madame Gory, have gone to Chicago for a week of the grand opera.

Born of all this, you would have thought that young Giddy would grow up a somewhat objectionable young man; and so, in fact, he did, though not nearly so objectionable as he might well have been, considering things in general and his mother in particular. At sixteen, for example, Giddy was driving his own car—a car so exaggerated and low-slung and with such a long predatory and glittering nose that one marveled at the expertness with which he swung its slim length around the corners of our narrow tree-shaded streets. He was a real Gory, was Giddy, with his thick waving black hair (which he tried for vain years to train into docility), his lean swart face, and his slightly hooked Gory nose. In appearance Winnebago pronounced him foreign looking—an attribute which he later turned into a doubtful asset in Nice. On the rare occasions when Giddy graced Winnebago with his presence you were likely to find him pursuing the pleasures that occupied other Winnebago boys of his age, if not station. In some miraculous way he had escaped being a snob. Still, training and travel combined to lead him into many innocent errors. When he dropped into Fetzer's pool shack carrying a malacca cane, for example. He had carried a cane every day for six months in Paris, whence he had just returned. Now it was as much a part of his street attire as his hat—more, to be exact, for the hatless head had just then become the street mode. There was a good game of Kelly in progress. Giddy, leaning slightly on his stick, stood watching it. Suddenly he was aware that all about the dim smoky little room players and loungers were standing in attitudes of exaggerated elegance. Each was leaning on a cue, his elbow crooked in as near an imitation of Giddy's position as the stick's length would permit. The figure was curved so that it stuck out behind and before; the expression on each face was as asinine as its owner's knowledge of the comic-weekly swell could make it; the little finger of the free hand was extravagantly bent. The players themselves walked with a mincing step about the table. And: "My deah fellah, what a pretty play. Mean to say, neat, don't you know," came incongruously from the lips of Reddy Lennigan, whose father ran the Lennigan House on Outagamie Street. He spatted his large hands delicately together in further expression of approval.

"Think so?" giggled his opponent, Mr. Dutchy Meisenberg. *"Aw*-fly sweet of you to say so, old thing." He tucked his unspeakable handkerchief up his cuff and coughed behind his palm. He turned to Giddy. "Excuse my not having my coat on, deah boy."

Just here Giddy might have done a number of things, all wrong. The game was ended. He walked to the table, and, using the offending stick as a cue, made a rather pretty shot that he had learned from Benoit in London. Then he ranged the cane neatly on the rack with the cues. He even grinned a little boyishly. "You win," he said. "My treat. What'll you have?"

Which was pretty sporting for a boy whose American training had been what Giddy's had been.

159

Giddy's father, on the death of old Gideon, proved himself much more expert at dispensing the paper mill money than at accumulating it. After old Madame Gory's death just one year following that of her husband, Winnebago saw less and less of the three remaining members of the royal family. The frame house on the river bluff would be closed for a year or more at a time. Giddy's father rather liked Winnebago and would have been content to spend six months of the year in the old Gory house, but Giddy's mother, who had been a Leyden, of New York, put that idea out of his head pretty effectively.

"Don't talk to me," she said, "about your duty toward the town that gave you your money and all that kind of feudal rot because you know you don't mean it. It bores you worse than it does me, really, but you like to think that the villagers are pulling a forelock when you walk down Normal Avenue. As a matter of fact they're not doing anything of the kind. They've got their thumbs to their noses, more likely."

Her husband protested rather weakly. "I don't care. I like the old shack. I know the heating apparatus is bum and that we get the smoke from the paper mills, but—I don't know—last year, when we had that punk pink palace at Cannes I kept thinking… "

Mrs. Gideon Gory raised the Leyden eyebrow. "Don't get sentimental, Gid, for God's sake! It's a shanty, and you know it. And you know that it needs everything from plumbing to linen. I don't see any sense in sinking thousands in making it livable when we don't want to live in it."

"But I do want to live in it—once in a while. I'm used to it. I was brought up in it. So was the kid. He likes it, too. Don't you, Giddy?" The boy was present, as usual, at this particular scene.

160

The boy worshipped his mother. But, also, he was honest. So, "Yeh, I like the ol' barn all right," he confessed.

Encouraged, his father went on: "Yesterday the kid was standing out there on the bluff-edge breathing like a whale, weren't you, Giddy? And when I asked him what he was puffing about he said he liked the smell of the sulphur and chemicals and stuff from the paper mills, didn't you, kid?"

Shame-facedly, "Yeh," said Giddy.

Betrayed thus by husband and adored son, the Leyden did battle. "You can both stay here, then," she retorted with more spleen than elegance, "and sniff sulphur until you're black in the face. I'm going to London in May."

They, too, went to London in May, of course, as she had known they would. She had not known, though, that in leading her husband to England in May she was leading him to his death as well.

"All Winnebago will be shocked and grieved to learn," said the Winnebago *Courier* to the extent of two columns and a cut, "of the sudden and violent death in England of her foremost citizen, Gideon Gory. Death was due to his being thrown from his horse while hunting."

To being thrown from his horse while hunting. Shocked and grieved though it might or might not be, Winnebago still had the fortitude to savour this with relish. Winnebago had died deaths natural and unnatural. It had been run over by automobiles, and had its skull fractured at football, and been drowned in Lake Winnebago, and struck by lightning, and poisoned by mushrooms, and shot by burglars. But never had a Winnebago citizen had the distinction of meeting death by

161

being thrown from his horse while hunting. While hunting. Scarlet coats. Hounds in full cry. Baronial halls. Hunt breakfasts. *Vogue. Vanity Fair.*

Well! Winnebago was almost grateful for this final and most picturesque gesture of Gideon Gory the second.

The widowed Leyden did not even take the trouble personally to superintend the selling of the Gory place on the river bluff. It was sold by an agent while she and Giddy were in Italy, and if she was ever aware that the papers in the transaction stated that the house had been bought by Orson J. Hubbell, she soon forgot the fact and the name. Giddy, leaning over her shoulder while she handled the papers, and signing on the line indicated by a legal forefinger, may have remarked:

"Hubbell. That's old Hubbell, the dray man. Must be money in the draying line."

Which was pretty stupid of him, because he should have known that the draying business was now developed into the motor truck business with great vans roaring their way between Winnebago and Kaukauna, Winnebago and Neenah, and even Winnebago and Oshkosh. He learned that later.

Just now Giddy wasn't learning much of anything, and, to do him credit, the fact distressed him not a little. His mother insisted that she needed him, and developed a bad heart whenever he rebelled and threatened to sever the apron-strings. They lived abroad entirely now. Mrs. Gory showed a talent for spending the Gory gold that must have set old Gideon to whirling in his Winnebago grave. Her spending of it was foolish enough, but her handling, of it was criminal. She loved Europe. America bored her. She wanted to identify herself with foreigners, with foreign life. Against advice she sold her large and lucrative interest in the Winnebago paper mills and invested great sums in French stocks, in Russian enterprises, in German shares.

She liked to be mistaken for a French woman.

She and Gideon spoke the language like natives — or nearly.

She was vain of Gideon's un-American looks, and cross with him when, on their rare and brief visits to New York, he insisted that he liked American tailoring and American-made shoes. Once or twice, soon after his father's death, he had said, casually, "You didn't like Winnebago, did you? Living in it, I mean."

"Like it!"

"Well, these English, I mean, and French — they sort of grow up in a place, and stay with it and belong to it, see what I mean? And it gives you a kind of permanent feeling. Not patriotic, exactly, but solid and native healthy and Scots-wha-hae-wi'-Wallace and all that kind of slop."

"Giddy darling, don't be silly."

Occasionally, too, he said, "Look here, Julia" — she liked this modern method of address — "look here, Julia, I ought to be getting busy. Doing something. Here I am, nineteen, and I can't do a thing except dance pretty well, but not as well as that South American eel we met last week; mix a cocktail pretty well, but not as good a one as Benny the bartender turns out at Voyot's; ride pretty well, but not as well as the English chaps; drive a car... "

She interrupted him there. "Drive a car better than even an Italian chauffeur. Had you there, Giddy darling."

She undoubtedly had Giddy darling there. His driving was little short of miraculous, and his feeling for the intricate inside of a motor engine was as delicate and unerring as that of a professional pianist for his pet pianoforte. They motored a good deal, with France as a permanent background and all Europe as a playground. They flitted about the continent, a whirl of glittering blue-and-cream enamel, tan leather coating, fur robes, air cushions, gold-topped flasks, and petrol. Giddy knew Como and Villa D'Este as the place where that pretty Hungarian widow had borrowed a thousand lires from him at the Casino roulette table and never paid him back; London as a pleasing potpourri of briar pipes, smart leather gloves, music-hall revues, and night clubs; Berlin as a rather stuffy hole where they tried to ape Paris and failed, but you had to hand it to Charlotte when it came to the skating at the Eis Palast. A pleasing existence, but unprofitable. No one saw the cloud gathering because of cloud there was none, even of the man's-hand size so often discerned as a portent.

When the storm broke (this must be hurriedly passed over because of the let's-not-talk-about-the-war-I'm-so-sick-of-it-aren't-you feeling) Giddy promptly went into the Lafayette Escadrille. Later he learned never to mention this to an American because the American was so likely to say, "There must have been about eleven million scrappers in that outfit. Every fella you meet's been in the Lafayette Escadrille. If all the guys were in it that say they were they could have licked the Germans the first day out. That outfit's worse than the old Floradora Sextette."

Mrs. Gory was tremendously proud of him, and not as worried as she should have been. She thought it all a rather smart game, and not at all serious. She wasn't even properly alarmed about her European money, at first. Giddy looked thrillingly distinguished and handsome in his aviation uniform. When she walked in the Paris streets with him she glowed like a girl with her lover. But after the first six months of it Mrs. Gory, grown rather drawn and haggard, didn't think the whole affair quite so delightful. She scarcely ever saw Giddy. She never heard the drum of an airplane without getting a sick, gone feeling at the pit of her stomach. She knew, now, that there was more to the air service than a becoming uniform. She was doing some war work herself in an incompetent, frenzied sort of way. With Giddy soaring high and her foreign stocks and bonds falling low she might well be excused for the panic that shook her from the time she opened her eyes in the morning until she tardily closed them at night.

"Let's go home, Giddy darling," like a scared child.

"Where's that?"

"Don't be cruel. America's the only safe place now."

"Too darned safe!" This was 1915.

By 1917 she was actually in need of money. But, Giddy did not know much about this because Giddy had, roughly speaking, got his. He had the habit of soaring up into the sunset and sitting around in a large pink cloud like a kid bouncing on a feather bed. Then, one day, he soared higher and farther than he knew, having, perhaps, grown careless through over-confidence. He heard nothing above the roar of his own engine, and the two planes were upon him almost before he knew it. They were not French, or English, or American planes. He got one of them and would have got clean away if the other had not caught him in the arm. The right arm. His mechanician lay

165

limp. Even then he might have managed a landing but the pursuing plane got in a final shot. There followed a period of time that seemed to cover, say, six years but that was actually only a matter of seconds. At the end of that period Giddy, together with a tangle of wire, silk, wood, and something that had been the mechanician, lay inside the German lines, and you would hardly have thought him worth the disentangling.

They did disentangle him, though, and even patched him up pretty expertly, but not so expertly, perhaps, as they might have, being enemy surgeons and rather busy with the patching of their own injured. The bone, for example, in the lower right arm, knitted promptly and properly, being a young and healthy bone, but they rather overlooked the matter of arm nerves and muscles, so that later, though it looked a perfectly proper arm, it couldn't lift four pounds. His head had emerged slowly, month by month, from swathings of gauze. What had been quite a crevasse in his skull became only a scarlet scar that his hair pretty well hid when he brushed it over the bad place. But the surgeon, perhaps being overly busy, or having no real way of knowing that Giddy's nose had been a distinguished and aristocratically hooked Gory nose, had remolded that wrecked feature into a pure Greek line at first sight of which Giddy stood staring weakly into the mirror; reeling a little with surprise and horror and unbelief and general misery. "Can this be I?" he thought, feeling like the old man of the bramble bush in the Mother Goose rhyme. A well-made and becoming nose, but not so fine looking as the original feature had been, as worn by Giddy.

"Look here!" he protested to the surgeon, months too late. "Look here, this isn't my nose."

"Be glad," replied that practical Prussian person, "that you have any."

166

With his knowledge of French and English and German Giddy acted as interpreter during the months of his invalidism and later internment, and things were not so bad with him. He had no news of his mother, though, and no way of knowing whether she had news of him. With 1918, and the Armistice and his release, he hurried to Paris and there got the full impact of the past year's events.

Julia Gory was dead and the Gory money nonexistent.

Out of the ruins — a jewel or two and some paper not quite worthless — he managed a few thousand francs and went to Nice. There he walked in the sunshine, and sat in the sunshine, and even danced in the sunshine, a dazed young thing together with hundreds of other dazed young things, not thinking, not planning, not hoping. Existing only in a state of semi-consciousness like one recovering from a blinding blow. The francs dribbled away. Sometimes he played baccarat and won; oftener he played baccarat and lost. He moved in a sort of trance, feeling nothing. Vaguely he knew that there was a sort of Conference going on in Paris. Sometimes he thought of Winnebago, recalling it remotely, dimly, as one is occasionally conscious of a former unknown existence. Twice he went to Paris for periods of some months, but he was unhappy there and even strangely bewildered, like a child. He was still sick in mind and body, though he did not know it. Driftwood, like thousands of others, tossed up on the shore after the storm; lying there bleached and useless and battered.

Then, one day in Nice, there was no money. Not a franc. Not a centime. He knew hunger. He knew terror. He knew desperation. It was out of this period that there emerged Giddy, the gigolo. Now, though, the name bristled with accent marks, thus: Gedeon Gore.

This Gedeon Gore, of the Nice dansants, did not even remotely resemble Gideon Gory of Winnebago, Wisconsin. This Gedeon Gore wore French clothes of the kind that Giddy Gory had always despised. A slim, sallow, sleek, sad-eyed gigolo in tight French garments, the pants rather flappy at the ankle; effeminate French shoes with fawn-coloured uppers and patent-leather eyelets and vamps, most despicable; a slim cane; hair with a magnificent natural wave that looked artificially marcelled and that was worn with a strip growing down from the temples on either side in the sort of cut used only by French dandies and English stage butlers. No, this was not Giddy Gory. The real Giddy Gory lay in a smart but battered suitcase under the narrow bed in his lodgings. The suitcase contained:

Item; one grey tweed suit with name of a London tailor inside.

Item; one pair Russia calf oxfords of American make.

Item; one French aviation uniform with leather coat, helmet, and gloves all bearing stiff and curious splotches of brown or rust-colour which you might not recognize as dried blood stains.

Item; one handful assorted medals, ribbons, orders, etc.

All Europe was dancing. It seemed a death dance, grotesque, convulsive, hideous. Paris, Nice, Berlin, Budapest, Rome, Vienna, London writhed and twisted and turned and jiggled. St. Vitus himself never imagined contortions such as these. In the narrow side-street dance rooms of Florence, and in the great avenue restaurants of Paris they were performing exactly the same gyrations — wiggle, squirm, shake. And over all the American jazz music boomed and whanged its syncopation. On the music racks of violinists who had meant to be Elmans or Kreislers were sheets entitled Jazz Baby Fox Trot. Drums, horns, cymbals, castanets, sandpaper. So the mannequins and marionettes of Europe tried to whirl themselves into forgetfulness.

The Americans thought Giddy was a Frenchman. The French knew him for an American, dress as he would. Dancing became with him a profession — no, a trade. He danced flawlessly, holding and guiding his partner impersonally, firmly, expertly in spite of the weak right arm — it served well enough. Gideon Gory had always been a naturally rhythmic dancer. Then, too, he had been fond of dancing. Years of practice had perfected him. He adopted now the manner and position of the professional. As he danced he held his head rather stiffly to one side, and a little down, the chin jutting out just a trifle. The effect was at the same time stiff and chic. His footwork was infallible. The intricate and imbecilic steps of the day he performed in flawless sequence. Under his masterly guidance the feet of the least rhythmic were suddenly endowed with deftness and grace. One swayed with him as naturally as with an elemental force. He danced politely and almost wordlessly unless first addressed, according to the code of his kind. His touch was firm, yet remote. The dance concluded, he conducted his partner to her seat, bowed stiffly from the waist, heels together, and departed. For these services he was handed ten francs, twenty francs, thirty francs, or more, if lucky, depending on the number of times he was called upon to dance with a partner during the evening. Thus was dancing, the most spontaneous and un-artificial of the Muses, vulgarized, commercialized, prostituted. Lower than Gideon Gory, of Winnebago, Wisconsin, had fallen, could no man fall.

Sometimes he danced in Paris. During the high season he danced in Nice. Afternoon and evening found him busy in the hot, perfumed, overcrowded dance salons. The Negresco,

169

the Ruhl, Maxim's, Belle Meuniere, the Casina Municipale. He learned to make his face go a perfect blank — pale, cryptic, expressionless. Between himself and the other boys of his ilk there was little or no professional comradeship. A weird lot they were, young, though their faces were strangely lacking in the look of youth. All of them had been in the war. Most of them had been injured. There was Aubin, the Frenchman. The left side of Aubin's face was rather startlingly handsome in its Greek perfection. It was like a profile chiseled. The left side was another face — the same, and yet not the same. It was as though you saw the left side out of drawing, or blurred, or out of focus. It puzzled you — shocked you. The left side of Aubin's face had been done over by an army surgeon who, though deft and scientific, had not had a hand expert as that of the Original Sculptor. Then there was Mazzetti, the Roman. He parted his hair on the wrong side, and under the black wing of it was a deep groove into which you could lay a forefinger. A piece of shell had plowed it neatly. The Russian boy who called himself Orloff had the look in his eyes of one who has seen things upon which eyes never should have looked. He smoked constantly and ate, apparently, not at all. Among these there existed a certain unwritten code and certain unwritten signals.

You did not take away the paying partner of a fellow gigolo. If in too great demand you turned your surplus partners over to gigolos unemployed. You did not accept less than ten francs (they all broke this rule). Sometimes Gedeon Gore made ten francs a day, sometimes twenty, sometimes fifty, infrequently a hundred. Sometimes not enough to pay for his one decent meal a day. At first he tried to keep fit by walking a certain number of miles daily along the ocean front. But usually he was too weary to persist in this. He did not think at all. He felt nothing. Sometimes, down deep, deep in a long-forgotten part of his being a voice called feebly, plaintively to the man who had been Giddy Gory. But he shut his ears and mind and consciousness and would not listen.

The American girls were best, the gigolos all agreed, and they paid well, though they talked too much. Gedeon Gore was a favourite among them. They thought he was so foreign looking, and kind of sad and stern and everything. His French, fluent, colloquial, and bewildering, awed them. They would attempt to speak to him in halting and hackneyed phrases acquired during three years at Miss Pence's Select School at Hastings-on-the-Hudson. At the cost of about a thousand dollars a word they would enunciate, painfully:

"Je pense que — um — *que Nice est le plus belle* — uh — *ville de France."*

Giddy, listening courteously, his head inclined as though unwilling to miss one conversational pearl falling from the pretty American's lips, would appear to consider this gravely. Then, sometimes in an unexpected burst of pure mischief, he would answer:

"You said something! *Some* burg, I'm telling the world."

The girl, startled, would almost leap back from the confines of his arms only to find his face stern, immobile, his eyes somber and reflective.

"Why! Where did you pick that up?"

His eyebrows would go up. His face would express complete lack of comprehension. *"Pardon?"*

171

Afterward, at home, in Toledo or Kansas City or Los Angeles, the girl would tell about it. "I suppose some American girl taught it to him, just for fun. It sounded too queer — because his French was so wonderful. He danced divinely. A Frenchman, and so aristocratic! Think of his being a professional partner. They have them over there, you know. Everybody's dancing in Europe. And gay! Why, you'd never know there'd been a war."

Mary Hubbell, of the Winnebago Hubbells, did not find it so altogether gay. Mary Hubbell, with her father, Orson J. Hubbell, and her mother, Bee Hubbell, together with what appeared to be practically the entire white population of the United States, came to Europe early in 1922, there to travel, to play, to rest, to behold, and to turn their good hard American dollars into cordwood-size bundles of German marks, Austrian kronen, Italian lires, and French francs. Most of the men regarded Europe as a wine list. In their mental geography Rheims, Rhine, Moselle, Bordeaux, Champagne, or Wurzburg were not localities but libations. The women, for the most part, went in for tortoise-shell combs, fringed silk shawls, jade earrings, beaded bags, and coral neck chains. Up and down the famous thoroughfare of Europe went the absurd pale blue tweed tailleurs and the lavender tweed cape suits of America's wives and daughters. Usually, after the first month or two, they shed these respectable, middle-class habiliments for what they fondly believed to be smart Paris costumes; and you could almost invariably tell a good, moral, church-going matron of the Middle West by the fact that she was got up like a demimondaine of the second class, in the naive belief that she looked French and chic.

The three Hubbells were thoroughly nice people. Mary Hubbell was more than thoroughly nice. She was a darb. She had done a completely good job during the 1918-1918 period, including the expert driving of a wild and unbroken Ford up and down the shell-torn roads of France. One of those smalltown girls with a big-town outlook, a well-trained mind, a slim boyish body, a good clear skin, and a steady eye that saw. Mary Hubbell wasn't a beauty by a good many measurements, but she had her points, as witness the number of bouquets, bundles, books, and bon-bons piled in her cabin when she sailed.

The well-trained mind and the steady seeing eye enabled Mary Hubbell to discover that Europe wasn't so gay as it seemed to the blind; and she didn't write home to the effect that you'd never know there'd been war.

The Hubbells had the best that Europe could afford. Orson J. Hubbell, a mild-mannered, grey-haired man with a nice flat waist-line and a good keen eye (hence Mary's) adored his women-folk and spoiled them. During the first years of his married life he had been Hubbell, the drayman, as Giddy Gory had said. He had driven one of his three drays himself, standing sturdily in the front of the red-painted wooden two-horse wagon as it rattled up and down the main business thoroughfare of Winnebago. But the war and the soaring freight-rates had dealt generously with Orson Hubbell. As railroad and shipping difficulties increased the Hubbell draying business waxed prosperous. Factories, warehouses, and wholesale business firms could be assured that their goods would arrive promptly, safely, and cheaply when conveyed by a Hubbell van. So now the three red-painted wooden horse-driven drays were magically transformed into a great fleet of monster motor vans that plied up and down the state of Wisconsin and even into Michigan and Illinois and Indiana. The Orson J. Hubbell Transportation Company, you read. And below, in yellow lettering on the red background:

Have HUBBELL Do Your HAULING.

There was actually a million in it, and more to come. The buying of the old Gory house on the river bluff had been one of the least of Orson's feats. And now that house was honeycombed with sleeping porches and linen closets and enamel fittings and bathrooms white and glittering as an operating auditorium. And there were shower baths, and blue rugs, and great soft fuzzy bath towels and little white innocent guest towels embroidered with curly H's whose tails writhed at you from all corners.

Orson J. and Mrs. Hubbell had never been in Europe before, and they enjoyed themselves enormously. That is to say, Mrs. Orson J. did, and Orson, seeing her happy, enjoyed himself vicariously. His hand slid in and out of his inexhaustible pocket almost automatically now. And "How much?" was his favourite locution. They went everywhere, did everything. Mary boasted a pretty fair French. Mrs. Hubbell conversed in the various languages, of Europe by speaking pidgin English very loud, and omitting all verbs, articles, adverbs, and other cumbersome superfluities. Thus, to the *file de chambre*.

"Me out now you beds." The red-cheeked one from the provinces understood, in some miraculous way, that Mrs. Hubbell was now going out and that the beds could be made and the rooms tidied.

They reached Nice in February and plunged into its gaieties. "Just think!" exclaimed Mrs. Hubbell rapturously, "only three francs for a facial or a manicure and two for a marcel. It's like finding them."

"If the Mediterranean gets any bluer," said Mary, "I don't think I can stand it, it's so lovely."

174

Mrs. Hubbell, at tea, expressed a desire to dance. Mary, at tea, desired to dance but didn't express it. Orson J. loathed tea; and the early draying business had somewhat unfitted his sturdy legs for the lighter movements of the dance. But he wanted only their happiness. So he looked about a bit, and asked some questions, and came back.

"Seems there's a lot of young chaps who make a business of dancing with the women-folks who haven't dancing men along. Hotel hires 'em. Funny to us but I guess it's all right, and quite the thing around here. You pay 'em so much a dance, or so much an afternoon. You girls want to try it?"

"I do," said Mrs. Orson J. Hubbell. "It doesn't sound respectable. Then that's what all those thin little chaps are who have been dancing with those pretty American girls. They're sort of ratty looking, aren't they? What do they call 'em? That's a nice-looking one, over there — no, no! — dancing with the girl in grey, I mean. If that's one I'd like to dance with him, Orson. Good land, what would the Winnebago ladies say! What do they call 'em, I wonder."

Mary had been gazing very intently at the nice looking one over there who was dancing with the girl in grey. She answered her mother's question, still gazing at him. "They call them gigolos," she said, slowly. Then, "Get that one Dad, will you, if you can? You dance with him first, Mother, and then I'll — "

"I can get two," volunteered Orson J.

"No," said Mary Hubbell, sharply.

The nice-looking gigolo seemed to be in great demand, but Orson J. succeeded in capturing him after the third dance. It turned out to be a tango, and though Mrs. Hubbell, pretty well

175

scared, declared that she didn't know it and couldn't dance it, the nice-looking gigolo assured her, through the medium of Mary's interpretation, that Mrs. Hubbell had only to follow his guidance. It was quite simple. He did not seem to look directly at Mary, or at Orson J. or at Mrs. Hubbell, as he spoke. The dance concluded, Mrs. Hubbell came back breathless, but enchanted.

"He has beautiful manners," she said, aloud, in English. "And dance! You feel like a swan when you're dancing with him. Try him, Mary." The gigolo's face, as he bowed before her, was impassive, inscrutable.

But, "Sh!" said Mary.

"Nonsense! Doesn't understand a word."

Mary danced the next dance with him. They danced wordlessly until the dance was half over. Then, abruptly, Mary said in English, "What's your name?"

Close against him she felt a sudden little sharp contraction of the gigolo's diaphragm — the contraction that reacts to surprise or alarm. But he said, in French, *"Pardon?"*

So, "What's your name?" said Mary, in French this time.

The gigolo with the beautiful manners hesitated longer than really beautiful manners should permit. But finally, "Je m'appelle Gedeon Gore." He pronounced it in his most nasal, perfect Paris French. It didn't sound even remotely like Gideon Gory.

"My name's Hubbell," said Mary, in her pretty fair French. "Mary Hubbell. I come from a little town called Winnebago."

The Gore eyebrow expressed polite disinterestedness.

"That's in Wisconsin," continued Mary, "and I love it."

"Naturellement," agreed the gigolo, stiffly.

They finished the dance without further conversation. Mrs. Hubbell had the next dance. Mary the next. They spent the afternoon dancing, until dinner time. Orson J.'s fee, as he handed it to the gigolo, was the kind that mounted grandly into dollars instead of mere francs. The gigolo's face, as he took it, was not more inscrutable than Mary's as she watched him take it.

From that afternoon, throughout the next two weeks, if any girl as thoroughly fine as Mary Hubbell could be said to run after any man, Mary ran after that gigolo. At the same time one could almost have said that he tried to avoid her. Mary took a course of tango lessons, and urged her mother to do the same. Even Orson J. noticed it.

"Look here," he said, in kindly protest. "Aren't you getting pretty thick with this jigger?"

"Sociological study, Dad. I'm all right."

"Yeh, you're all right. But how about him?"

"He's all right, too."

The gigolo resisted Mary's unmaidenly advances, and yet, when he was with her, he seemed sometimes to forget to look somber and blank and remote. They seemed to have a lot to say to each other. Mary talked about America a good deal. About her home town . . . "and big elms and maples and oaks in the yard . . . the Fox River valley . . . Middle West . . . Normal Avenue . . . Cass Street . . . Fox River paper mills . . ."

She talked in French and English. The gigolo confessed, one day, to understanding some English, though he seemed to speak none. After that Mary, when very much in earnest, or when enthusiastic, spoke in her native tongue altogether. She claimed an intense interest in European after-war conditions, in reconstruction, in the attitude toward life of those millions of young men who had actually participated in the conflict. She asked questions that might have been considered impertinent, not to say nervy.

"Now you," she said, brutally, "are a person of some education, refinement, and background. Yet you are content to dance around in these — these — well, back home a chap might wash dishes in a cheap restaurant or run an elevator in an east side New York loft building, but he'd never —"

A very faint dull red crept suddenly over the pallor of the gigolo's face. They were sitting out on a bench on the promenade, facing the ocean (in direct defiance on Mary's part of all rules of conduct of respectable girls toward gigolos). Mary Hubbell had said rather brusque things before. But now, for the first time, the young man defended himself faintly.

"For us," he replied in his exquisite French, "it is finished. For us there is nothing. This generation, it is no good. I am no good. They are no good." He waved a hand in a gesture that included the promenaders, the musicians in the cafes, the dancers, the crowds eating and drinking at the little tables lining the walk.

"What rot!" said Mary Hubbell, briskly. "They probably said exactly the same thing in Asia after Alexander had got through with 'em. I suppose there was such dancing and general devilment in Macedonia that every one said the younger generation had gone to the dogs since the war, and the world would never amount to anything again. But it seemed to pick up, didn't it?"

The boy turned and looked at her squarely for the first time, his eyes meeting hers. Mary looked at him. She even swayed toward him a little, her lips parted. There was about her a breathlessness, an expectancy. So they sat for a moment, and between them the air was electric, vibrant. Then, slowly, he relaxed, sat back, slumped a little on the bench. Over his face, that for a moment had been alight with something vital, there crept again a look of defeat, of somber indifference. At sight of that look Mary Hubbell's jaw set. She leaned forward. She clasped her fine large hands tight, did not look at the gigolo, but out, across the Mediterranean, and beyond it. Her voice was and a little tremulous and she spoke in English only.

"It isn't finished here — here in Europe. But it's sick. Back home, in America, though, it's alive. Alive! And growing. I wish I could make understand what it's like there. It's all new, crude, maybe, and ugly, but it's so darned healthy and sort of clean. I love it. I love every bit of it. I know I sound like a flag-waver but I don't care. I mean it. And I know it's sentimental, but I'm proud of it. The kind of thing I feel about United States is the kind of thing Mencken sneers at. You don't know who Mencken is. He's a critic who pretends to despise everything because he's really a sentimentalist and afraid somebody'll find it out. I don't say I don't appreciate the beauty of all this Italy and France and England and Germany. But it doesn't get me the way just the mention of a name will get me back home. This trip, for example. Why, last summer four of us — three other girls and I — motored from Wisconsin to California, and we drove every inch of the way ourselves. The Santa Fe Trail!

179

The Ocean-to-Ocean Highway! The Lincoln Highway! The Dixie Highway! The Yellowstone Trail! The very sound of those words gives me a sort of prickly feeling. They mean something so big and vital and new. I get a thrill out of them that I haven't had once over here. Why even this," she threw out a hand that included and dismissed the whole sparkling panorama before her, "this doesn't begin to give the jolt that I got out of Walla Walla, and Butte, and Missoula, and Spokane, and Seattle, and Albuquerque. We drove all day, and ate ham and eggs at some little hotel or lunch-counter at night, and outside the hotel the drummers would be sitting, talking and smoking; and there were Western men, very tanned and tall and lean, in those big two-gallon hats and khaki pants and puttees. And there were sunsets, and sand, and cactus and mountains, and campers and Fords. I can smell the Kansas corn fields and I can see the Iowa farms and the ugly little raw American towns, and the big thin American men, and the grain elevators near the railroad stations, and I know those towns weren't the way towns ought to look. They were ugly and crude and new. Maybe it wasn't all beautiful, but gosh! It was real, and growing, and big and alive! Alive!"

Mary Hubbell was crying. There, on the bench along the promenade in the sunshine at Nice, she was crying.

The boy beside her suddenly rose, uttered a little inarticulate sound, and left her there on the bench in the sunshine. Vanished, completely, in the crowd.

For three days the Orson J. Hubbells did not see their favourite gigolo. If Mary was disturbed she did not look it, though her eye was alert in the throng. During the three days of their gigolo's absence Mrs. Hubbell and Mary availed themselves of the professional services of the Italian gigolo Mazzetti. Mrs. Hubbell said she thought his dancing was, if

180

anything, more nearly perfect than that What's-his-name, but his manner wasn't so nice and she didn't like his eyes. Sort of sneaky. Mary said she thought so, too.

Nevertheless she was undoubtedly affable toward him, and talked (in French) and laughed and even walked with him, apparently in complete ignorance of the fact that these things were not done. Mazzetti spoke frequently of his colleague, Gore, and always in terms of disparagement. A low fellow. A clumsy dancer. One unworthy of Mary's swanlike grace. Unfit to receive Orson J. Hubbell's generous fees.

Late one evening, during the mid-week after-dinner dance, Gore appeared suddenly in the doorway. It was ten o'clock. The Hubbells were dallying with their after-dinner coffee at one of the small tables about the dance floor.

Mary, keen-eyed, saw him first. She beckoned Mazzetti who stood in attendance beside Mrs. Hubbell's chair. She snatched up the wrap that lay at hand and rose. "It's stifling in here. I'm going out on the Promenade for a breath of air. Come on." She plucked at Mazzetti's sleeve and actually propelled him through the crowd and out of the room. She saw Gore's startled eyes follow them.

She even saw him crossing swiftly to where her mother and father sat. Then she vanished into the darkness with Mazzetti. And the Mazzettis put but one interpretation upon a young woman who strolls into the soft darkness of the Promenade with a gigolo.

And Mary Hubbell knew this.

Gedeon Gore stood before Mr. and Mrs. Orson J. Hubbell. "Where is your daughter?" he demanded, in French.

181

"Oh, howdy-do," chirped Mrs. Hubbell. "Well, it's Mr. Gore! We missed you. I hope you haven't been sick."

"Where is your daughter?" demanded Gedeon Gore, in French. "Where is Mary?"

Mrs. Hubbell caught the word Mary. "Oh, Mary. Why, she's gone out for a walk with Mr. Mazzetti."

"Good God!" said Gedeon Gore, in perfectly plain English. And vanished.

Orson J. Hubbell sat a moment, thinking. Then, "Why, say, he talked English. That young French fella talked English."

The young French fella, hatless, was skimming down the Promenade des Anglais, looking intently ahead, and behind, and to the side, and all around in the darkness. He seemed to be following a certain trail, however. At one side of the great wide walk, facing the ocean, was a canopied bandstand. In its dim shadow, he discerned a wisp of white. He made for it, swiftly, silently. Mazzetti's voice low, eager, insistent. Mazzetti's voice hoarse, ugly, importunate. The figure in white rose. Gore stood before the two. The girl took a step toward him, but Mazzetti took two steps and snarled like a villain in a movie, if a villain in a movie could be heard to snarl.

"Get out of here!" said Mazzetti, in French, to Gore. "You pig! Swine! To intrude when I talk with a lady. You are finished. Now she belongs to me."

"The hell she does!" said Giddy Gory in perfectly plain American and swung for Mazzetti with his bad right arm. Mazzetti, after the fashion of his kind, let fly in most unsportsmanlike fashion with his feet, kicking at Giddy's stomach and trying to bite with his small sharp yellow teeth. And then Giddy's left, that had learned some neat tricks of boxing in the days of the Gory greatness, landed fairly on the Mazzetti nose. And with a howl of pain and rage and terror the Mazzetti, a hand clapped to that bleeding feature, fled in the darkness.

And, "Oh, Giddy!" said Mary, "I thought you'd never come."

"Mary. Mary Hubbell. Did you know all the time? You did, didn't you? You think I'm a bum, don't you? Don't you?"

Her hand on his shoulder. "Giddy, I've been stuck on you since I was nine years old, in Winnebago. I kept track of you all through the war, though I never once saw you. Then I lost you. Giddy, when I was a kid I used to look at you from the sidewalk through the hedge of the house on Cass. Honestly. Honestly, Giddy."

"But look at me now. Why, Mary, I'm — I'm no good. Why, I don't see how you ever knew —"

"It takes more than a new Greek nose and French clothes and a bum arm to fool me, Gid. Do you know, there were a lot of photographs of you left up in the attic of the Cass Street house when we bought it? I know them all by heart, Giddy. By heart . . . Come on home, Giddy. Let's go home."